Through The Eyes Of God

M. David Smith

This work is of fiction. Names, characters, places and incidents either are the product of the author's imagination or are used fictitiously. Any resemblances to actual persons, living or dead, events, or locales is entirely coincidental.

Copyright © 2020 by Matthew David Smith

All rights reserved. Not part of the book may be used in any matter without written permission of the copyright owner except for the use of quotations in book review.

Front and back cover design by Grace Boden

Edited by Grace Boden

To Grace,

for all your work, help, support,
encouragement, and above all else, patience.

Contents

Opening..................................1
Chapter 2................................10
Chapter 3................................26
Chapter 4................................43
Chapter 5................................64
Chapter 6................................79
Chapter 7................................93
Chapter 8................................112
Chapter 9................................131
Chapter 10..............................146
Chapter 11..............................163
Chapter 12..............................185
Chapter 13..............................206
Chapter 14..............................221
Chapter 15..............................235
Chapter 16..............................256
Chapter 17..............................265
Chapter 18..............................278
Chapter 19..............................294
Conclusion.............................307

Opening

Jacob stood above the desk, gazing down upon the work that had encapsulated and consumed the last month of his life. The light of the mid afternoon sun shone through the window like a spotlight. The sunlight poured onto the unkempt mess of pencil and eraser shavings scattered across the surface of his desk. Resting at his feet were several pencils, each one sharpened down to a nub. Hidden underneath the debris was an assortment of papers. Each page provided a glimpse into a rather extraordinary revelation. A story, not one of fiction, at least according to the writer, but instead one of a personal experience. An account that seemed to provide an answer to one of life's unending questions. The answer given, or to be more accurate, revealed, through rather unorthodox means.

    Looking upon his writings he was uncertain as to what his next step should be. He had been given not only a revelation into a question that had persisted in his mind for most of his life, but also an assignment to provide an answer to those asking the very same question.

    Despite knowing what he was called to do, there was a lingering doubt in his mind that the direction he was given was genuine. After a few moments of contemplation he gathered each page, cleaned off the assortment of pencil and eraser shavings, and quickly sorted the papers into the order that would tell his story. He carefully stapled them together, and with a deep breath he closed the curtains and turned to walk out the door into the hallway of his home. The sound of the door shutting behind him broke the silence that would otherwise occupy his house during this time of the day. He was completely alone that Sunday afternoon, despite living with his parents and older sister. For the last two months silence in his home had not been a rare occurrence.

    He descended the stairs toward the front door, the papers still firmly gripped in his right hand. As Jacob reached the bottom step, he slipped his hand into his left pants pocket and pulled out a set of keys. He fumbled through them and after a few seconds he managed to locate the key to the front door of his house. Before walking through the door, Jacob turned towards the bottom of the open closet to his right while slipping on his shoes; a habit he had fallen into without even realizing. Near the back of the closet, tucked away yet still visible, was a small pair of shoes. They were broken in, yet barely worn. They no longer fit anyone in his house. They were a remnant of the past, something that Jacob's family had clung to and refused to let go of. He let out a sombre *sigh* before finally closing the closet.

    Jacob turned the deadbolt lock on the door before walking out towards the street in front of his home. He had grown up in that neighbourhood and had spent countless hours creating memories of playing in those very same streets with his childhood friends. It seemed that no matter how many times he walked through his community there was always a sense of nostalgia that he couldn't seem to ignore. He often found himself yearning to return to the innocent days of his youth. Despite the nostalgia that he felt, he was entirely aware that he was simply viewing those memories through rose-tinted glasses.

As Jacob made his way down the path he had walked countless times before, two young children, a boy and a girl, sitting at the bottom of a driveway across the street caught his attention. Each one was surrounded by an assortment of different coloured chalk, which they had used to turn the black asphalt driveway into their own personal canvas. A mess of various colours and shapes, yet a masterpiece in their eyes all the same. Their own world lay in front of them, a world they themselves created, one to shape and mould to their own desire. Sitting in front of the house, adjacent to the driveway were an elderly couple, the children's grandparents presumably. As Jacob continued to walk he began to think about their lives. The individual choices they had made, the relationships they had formed. The culmination of experiences they had lived through, all of which led them to that exact moment.

He had found himself doing this quite frequently. All too often he'd find himself getting lost thinking about the lives of others, trying to imagine the journeys they had taken, thinking about the stories they could all tell. A rather unusual way of looking at the world, yet it's something he had instinctively and frequently done over the course of the last month. A thought with far greater perspective than those of his peers, yet it was a question that he found himself asking time and time again. An enlightened perspective rooted in his revelation, and the underlying foundation of the story gripped in his hand.

The brief glimpse into the lives of those around us is only but a fraction of their journey as a whole. Jacob understood this, as well as the myriad of paths and opportunities that would remain unseen, and the unrealized possibilities that lay before each and every person. Yet it often seemed as though the paths so many walked down and the experiences they endured were unjust and undeserved.

The question as to why such a dark reality can exist would eventually lay as the basis for Jacob's revelation, and the answer he sought. This would eventually bestow him with a revelation that opened his eyes to the true complexity and depth of the world and of the lives of those around him.

As Jacob's focus remained elsewhere, his body managed to find its way to the destination he had initially set out to reach. Standing before him was the local church he and his family had attended for as long as he could recall. Sitting inside of the building was the church's pastor; an elderly man, who had been anticipating this day, this meeting with Jacob, for some time now. As Jacob walked towards the front doors, the reflected image he saw of himself in the glass panels began to transition into a lens displaying the interior of the church. He reached out to the brass coloured door handles to let himself into the building, a motion he had done countless times before.

    Jacob took a moment to take in his surroundings before making his way down to the pastor's office. The emptiness of the church was an unusual occurrence, it was a sight Jacob had rarely seen despite attending the church for so long. The main foyer that was so often crowded with members of his community during Sunday mornings was eerily empty. The last remnants of the church's small staff and congregation had all left prior to Jacob's arrival. The foyer, which was normally flooded with the various conversations of the members of the church, the attendees, the volunteers and the staff, was all but silent.

    The necessity to watch his step for running children was gone, much to Jacob's relief. After indulging in the moment for a few seconds, Jacob began to make his way down a hall to the right of the sanctuary. With each step the grip he had on the papers in his right hand began to tighten as his nerves began to grow.

    Walking down the hall, he passed by the room that was dedicated to the children's Sunday school class, a room where he had spent most of his Sunday mornings during his childhood. Jacob and his siblings would attend their church's Sunday school class with only a handful of other children. It was there he had learned the basics of God, Jesus, and some of the more accessible Biblical stories.

However, the children's class was also where the most important questions relating to God were asked. Not as a means to disprove, or argue with the teachers, but instead with genuine, innocent curiosity. Every week as the lesson concluded, the teachers, often young adults in their early twenties, would ask the children if they had anything they would like prayer for. More often than not, their requests were typical for children their age; prayer for upcoming tests, friends who were sick, safety for their family, among others.

Despite the immaturity of the children, their requests always had an authenticity and humanity to them. But in asking for those prayers, questions relating to those very issues were often asked. "Why won't God heal my friend who got sick?" or "Why won't God help me do better in school?" Questions, innocent in nature, but the complexity of the subject of theodicy was beyond the expertise of the teachers, and the comprehension of the children.

Often the teachers would reference Biblical examples as a means to provide the children with an answer they could accept. Frequently, the teachers' answers would cite theological examples pertaining to the children's questions,"If Jesus was able to heal people, then wouldn't that mean that God can heal your friend?"

The answer always made sense as a child, yet as Jacob grew up, he saw it as nothing more than a cop out; a means for the young adult teachers to cover their own lack of understanding while simultaneously instilling the children with faith in God. He couldn't blame them, really. Understanding why the world is so full of pain is difficult, and the lack of a clear answer is exactly what caused him to reach his breaking point. However, those very same unanswered questions laid the foundation for his experience, and the revelation that brought him back to the church he had briefly left.

The sound of each of his footsteps began to echo down the hall as he neared the pastor's office. Jacob stood in front of the door for a moment, uncertain about what he was about to do, about what he knew he was called to do. In front of him was the door to the pastor's office, on it was a placard marked *'Pastor William Peterson'*. Jacob lifted up his left hand to the door, which remained hovering in front of it, frozen in place by a mixture of hesitation and nervousness. Before Jacob was able to decide his next action, he heard a familiar voice coming from behind.

"No need to knock, there is no one inside."

He quickly turned to find himself face-to-face with his church's pastor. Pastor William, an elderly man, dressed in a clean grey suit, one fitting the head of a church, stood behind him.

"I have been waiting for this day for a quite a while. Please take a seat inside." Pastor William said, a lilt of anticipation filled his voice.

"Thanks," Jacob nervously responded before reaching for the doorknob and gently twisting it, allowing himself and the pastor into the office.
Jacob sat down in one of two chairs facing a desk sitting in the middle of the room. The pastor followed soon after, slowly pulling the chair out from his desk before sitting down and centring himself in front of Jacob.

"So, tell me about this experience of yours."

2

"I don't even know where to begin," Jacob said nervously, "I have no idea if what happened was real, or some sort of weird hallucination. Everything felt so real, but I also felt like I was outside of, well, reality. It sounds confusing, I know. It's something that I've been struggling to understand myself for the better part of the last month. Even now, I'm still trying to make sense of it all. But as strange as it seems, I don't think I really need to fully understand exactly what happened."

"What do you mean by that?" the pastor asked.

"It's so strange. For so long I tried to

understand my life, who I was, why everything felt so beyond my control. I had so many questions that went unanswered. Despite my confusion it all eventually started to make sense to me. God gave me a revelation, not just for me, but also for others like me. Ever since that day I felt as though God was calling me to write this."

Jacob lifted up the pile of papers still gripped in his right hand and placed them on top of the desk. The pastor looked down at the papers in confusion, then he picked them up and began to flip through the pages before looking back up towards Jacob.

"What is this?" The pastor inquired curiously.

"It's the revelation God gave me. I know you wanted to hear about my experience first hand, but I don't believe that's how God wants me to tell my story. I want you to take the time to read it for yourself. To not just understand the experience God gave me, but to understand the life I've lived that led up to that moment. I think God wants to speak to others who have struggled in the same ways I did, and I believe He's going to use this story to do just that. All I ask is that you share my story with anyone you know who might be struggling as I was."

"I understand," The pastor said as he placed the papers back down onto his desk. "If this is truly God's will, who am I to argue? Is there anything else you would like to talk about?"

"No, I think that's about it. Thank you for taking the time to meet with me." Jacob said graciously before standing up from his chair.

"It was my pleasure," The pastor stood up and reached out to shake Jacob's hand.

After a firm handshake, Jacob turned towards the door before opening it and letting himself back out into the hallway of the church.

"That was rather fast." Pastor William muttered to himself as he sat back down into his chair. His eyes focused on the pile of papers in front of him. Sitting on top was a single sheet, one almost entirely blank except for two hand written words: *'My Story'* written perfectly in the middle, and the name *'Jacob Stame'* written directly underneath the title. Pastor William lifted up the papers from his desk and began to flip through the pages once more before turning his attention back to the title. After turning the title page over he was met with a messy assortment of hand written paragraphs. Nothing illegible, yet not the clearest penmanship he had seen either. Despite the disorderly penmanship, Pastor William still had an appreciation for the written word over printed text.

Written in the middle, atop the second page was the word *'Introduction'*. A simple, yet self-explanatory title about what was to come. Beneath the title was an inside look at someone's life, a lens into a life no one had known other than Jacob himself. Internal struggles that never saw the light of day, ongoing battles with his own emotions that he had always remained silent about. A mind flooded by unanswerable questions of fairness, faith, purpose and meaning. A chaotic inner turmoil which no one had any indication even existed.

Pastor William focused his eyes on the beginning of the paragraph as he began to read the story of Jacob's life. A story that was hidden within someone he had known for many years. However, despite the length of their relationship, the details of Jacob's life remained beyond pastor's knowledge. The life of someone who had seen the world through the eyes of God himself.

*

-Introduction-

I don't know who exactly I'm writing this for, or who is going to be reading this. Perhaps that answer will be revealed to me at a later time when this is all complete. This letter is not written as a means to tell some improbable fable, or to convince someone of a high power, one which I cannot even understand myself, let alone describe. No, this is simply a means for me to articulate what I have been through. It was an experience I'm still trying to comprehend, even to this very day; and one that will hopefully speak to at least one other person the same way it spoke to me.

For so long I sought God for an answer as to why exactly He would allow myself, and so many others to endure a life that felt so unjust. Why do so many people, of all walks of life, have to continually overcome trials that always feel beyond our own control? Unending loneliness and depression which so many people are trapped in, the incurable illnesses that have plagued humanity for centuries, and the random and senseless disasters that have claimed countless victims. The only conclusion that I could ever reach is that God either cared for a select few, or for none of us at all.

I was constantly told that God loved the world equally, but the troubles that we all faced always seemed to convey just the opposite. The endless stream of unanswerable questions over the years began to manifest into an anger towards God himself. Despite my prayers, despite genuinely seeking God, I felt as though I was entirely abandoned. I was unable to ignore the feeling in the back of my mind that I was screaming into the void, and that 'God' was simply a concept to give a false sense of hope to those in their times of emotional distress. In spite of my efforts to suppress such thoughts, I was unable to completely ignore their presence. I began to feel as though I was clinging to a false sense of hope, against the overwhelming flood of depression that would continually urge me to give up on God.

Despite how I may have felt, unbeknownst to me, God was listening. He had an answer for me, a revelation only He could provide. A revelation greater than I could have ever imagined, and one I'm not soon to forget. I desperately want to believe there's a reason for the revelation He gave me; a reason with greater purpose than for my own understanding of His will. I'm not a prophet from God and would never claim to have a greater understanding of His work. I simply feel called to share with the world the story of how God answered my prayers with a revelation beyond my own comprehension.

The revelation seemed to defy logic, yet provided me with greater insight into the nature of who God truly is. This is not meant to be an answer for every question surrounding God. Instead, this is the answer

He gave to me when I sought after Him. An answer to why I had to live through struggles that so often felt beyond my own control. Struggles that I had endured alone, yet were not exclusive to my own life. I was provided understanding to it all, but not through a passage in the Bible, or through a pastor's message. Instead, it was through God allowing me to see the world from His point of view. To see the world through the lens of the creator, through the eyes of God Himself.

I was the second child of three, born into an average middle class family; we were neither affluent nor needy. A life full of potential, full of opportunities, or at least that's how it would initially appear. My family was and still is a traditional, Christian family. A family whose foundation was built on our faith, faith in a God that I was told had laid out a path for all of our lives. A God who desired what's best for us, a God who listened to our prayers and would answer us in our times of need. There was always such tremendous comfort in believing that God would never leave us nor forsake us. Yet as I grew up I couldn't help but feel as though God had abandoned me.

Despite my unending cries to Him, I continually felt as though my prayers fell upon deaf ears. No matter how hard I sought after Him, no matter what book or verse I was studying in my Bible, it always felt as though He was just beyond my reach. This feeling of pessimism had formed contrary to a childhood upbringing that had initially instilled a more optimistic view of life. A childhood that was full of encouragement, full of faith that God would always be there for me despite the circumstances, despite my frustration and pain.

So often during my youth, myself, and so many others were told of the incredible possibilities that would eventually lay before us. It arose a sense of optimism in all our minds; the supposedly untapped potential that laid dormant within each of us. Our limitless childhood imagination, combined with the constant encouragement of those around us would lead us to believe we could achieve our greatest desires. As children we all began to envision our future. The incredible dreams and aspirations that dwelled within our minds felt entirely tangible and achievable, yet as time began to draw onward the realities of the world around us would slowly begin to humble those very dreams.

The constant reinforcement that my teachers would give us unfortunately had the exact opposite effect. To be told that I can accomplish anything if I were to set my mind to it, yet I constantly struggled to comprehend and process the lessons that they were so passionately teaching my class. I felt as though I didn't belong, that I was alone in my struggles, disconnected from those around me. Outwardly I appeared as happy and jovial as my classmates, yet internally I felt as though I was perpetually displaced.

Looking back on my own childhood I soon began to wonder if I was truly alone in those moments. If the unspoken difficulties and desire to feel equal to those around me was exclusive to myself, or if there were others who also struggled to feel as though they belonged. Perhaps there were others who, like me, portrayed a facade to hide their own insecurities in an attempt to feel equal to their peers.

However, in the midst of my own fruitless attempts to feel academically on par with my classmates, there existed a means for me to not only match, but to exceed those whom I felt were always beyond my reach. Even at an early age I always resonated with the more artistic related subjects in school. It was then that I began to experience a feeling that was otherwise so foreign to me, a feeling of confidence and self-assurance.

To a young child even the most outlandish creation would look like a masterpiece if made by their own hands, yet there always seemed to be a potential that those around me could see in my work. The feeling that I could excel in an area of school truly felt like a breath of fresh air in an otherwise suffocating environment. However, despite what I initially thought to be a means for me to finally surpass my peers, I soon began to realize that the more traditionally academic subjects were given greater priority over the only classes that instilled any sense of confidence and competence in me.

The festering emotions I experienced would have otherwise felt overwhelming if not for a singular refuge that existed in the form of my small group of friends, Richard, Amy and Michael. There were only a few of us, a close-knit group of friends who walked alongside each other during the entirety of our childhood and adolescence. It was during those times, in the presence of my friends, when I felt genuinely accepted and included. It was the moments we were all together that I felt the growing feeling of self-doubt and uncertainty fade into nothingness.

Despite our close bond, the four of us possessed drastically different personalities. Richard was theatrical, colourful and expressive, he lived as though the world itself was his own personal audience and he was their star. He was a natural showman to say the least. In direct contrast to him was Amy, a soft spoken, mild mannered girl, who not only epitomized a natural motherly tendency to care for others, but fully embraced it. She was someone who had always been willing to put others before herself, regardless of the situation.

Michael, despite being the same age as us, was someone we all looked up to. He was the type of child that, despite his young age, was as much a friend as he was a role model. Wise beyond his years, he possessed a strong moral compass and he always sought to do what he believed to be right. Lastly there was myself, a quiet child, one who was never too expressive, and one that found difficulty opening up to those around me. Yet, despite my noticeable lack of social skills, I still had friends who accepted me regardless. They were my solace and my escape in the midst of it all.

The sense of belonging that I felt with Richard, Michael and Amy gave me a feeling of comfort and acceptance that I revelled in, but never it took for granted. I would often see other children playing by themselves; those without friends, whether that be due to their own rather eccentric personalities, shyness, or simply by choice. Though I felt intellectually displaced among my peers, I remained thankful for those who considered me their friend.

While there are those who are content by themselves, many others desire to feel accepted by their peers, yet are unable to satisfy that yearning. It was during those precious times with my friends that I would experience that feeling of acceptance. However, despite the closeness of our group, I was still left to myself from time to time. Left to dwell in the growing self-doubt, a feeling which I desperately wish remained at school, but one that lingered inside of me even after the final bell would ring.

The times I spent at home arose similar feelings of uncertainty and insignificance, albeit for different reasons. Being the middle child my parents' attention seemed to be more focused towards my older sister Julia, and my younger brother Alexander, a common experience for middle children. I frequently felt as though my parents gave greater priority towards the needs of my siblings, over my own. I know my parents cared for me, but so often it felt as though I was an afterthought.

My older sister seemed to be the exact opposite of me in virtually every way. Everywhere I struggled, she excelled. My noticeable lack of social skills were in direct contrast to her optimistic, personable and charismatic personality. The limitless potential that I was taught we all had as children seemed to be completely attainable by her. From her academic achievements to her extracurricular activities, everything seemed to come naturally to her. Despite it all, I never had an ounce of animosity towards Julia. In fact, I too wanted to see her succeed. Yet in seeing her frequent success I couldn't help but feel as though I didn't live up to my parents' expectations.

I understood that my parents' expectations for me differed from those they had for Julia. However despite knowing this, I often felt that since I didn't live up to the expectations I placed upon myself in comparison to my sister, I was of lesser worth than her. I knew that to be a lie, yet it was one that remained embedded in the back of my mind throughout my childhood and even into adulthood.

Despite the frustration that I felt towards myself, Julia was always encouraging towards me. Perhaps it was because she was my older sister and therefore had a natural tendency to care for her younger brother, but I think there was more to it than that. I believe she knew what I was going through, even though I never actually admitted my inner struggles to anyone. It felt as though there was an unspoken understanding between her and I, a feeling that I really can't explain, yet one I couldn't seem to deny either. She wanted to see me do well, not for the sake of gaining the recognition that she'd often receive, but instead for myself. She wanted me to feel as though I had the value that she knew I had, even if I didn't know it at the time.

Alexander was my younger brother and given his place as the youngest he always seemed to have the majority of my parents attention, but it wasn't solely due to his age. Alexander was born with a medical condition, one I never truly understood at the time of his birth. My parents had always told me that God made him 'special'. I understand now that this was a simple and positive term to help me to accept something that was much more complex, certainly beyond my comprehension at that age. Unfortunately due to his condition, my needs were often overshadowed by those of Alexander's. I know this wasn't my parents intention. I knew that they loved and cared for me, but given the condition of my brother, their focus was all too often placed entirely on him while I was left alone.

Alexander's life was a struggle, one he was blissfully unaware of. Due to his condition Alexander was ever reliant on my parents, unable to fend for himself, unable to consciously understand the world around him. As his brother, I always felt an ever present need to protect and care for him, unfortunately due to my young age, there was very little I could actually do for him. Despite my efforts and prayers, I knew that any attempt to aid Alexander would have been entirely fruitless and ultimately in vain.

Despite feeling as though my needs were overshadowed by my siblings' I never held any ill will towards either Julia or Alexander. The support I received from Julia and the deep care I felt towards Alexander remained as beacons of light in my life. The love I felt for my family didn't alleviate me of the feelings that would soon feed into my own emotional struggles; a perpetually growing feeling of pessimism and frustration towards God and the life he had supposedly planned for me. A life that so often felt so unfair and undeserved, and one I struggled to accept as God's design.

*

It was at this time Pastor William took his eyes away from the papers in his hand and shifted his focus to the analog clock mounted on the wall of his office. The face of the clock read five-thirty. It was only then that he realized how quickly the afternoon had slipped by. He placed the papers back on his desk, stood up from his chair and slowly began to stretch out his stiffened arms. After pushing his chair back into its place in front of his desk, he once again picked up the papers and began to make his way to the door of his office.

He lifted his hand to the switch on the wall and turned off the lights allowing the room to be filled with darkness before finally walking through the door. The story was still fresh in his mind as he walked down the halls of his church. The main foyer was flooded with a deep orange light emitting from the now setting sun. Pastor William walked up to the door while pulling out a small set of keys from his pocket. The clink of the metallic keys while Pastor William located the one to the front doors broke the silence in the otherwise quiet room. As he walked through the doors the intensity of the orange sunset increased. He raised the papers in his hand, shielding his eyes from the sunlight as they slowly began to adjust from the artificial light in his office.

Just as he had done many times before, Pastor William inserted a key into the church's door and twisted it until he heard the familiar sound of the deadbolt sliding into place. With the doors to the church locked for the evening, Pastor William began to make his way to his car while still contemplating the story firmly gripped in his hand.

3

The car was silent during Pastor William's drive home from the church. The sound of the radio that would so often accompany him during his drive was entirely absent. The lack of ambient music allowed the pastor's mind to remain fixated on the pile of papers that lay on the passenger's seat next to him. Within those pages was documentation of a supposed God given revelation. Interpreting the revelations of God's influence in someone's life wasn't anything new to the pastor. On the contrary, it was an area that Pastor William had a considerable amount of experience. However, what perplexed the pastor was not the fact that Jacob had experienced an apparent divine revelation from God, but that he was perfectly content in not fully understanding the meaning and purpose behind his revelation.

It wasn't Jacob's passivity towards his own revelation that perplexed the pastor, instead it was Jacob's belief that his revelation was not for himself, but for others. This was in direct contrast to Pastor William's extensive experience in this area of discerning God's interventions, where the revelations were of personal self-reflection, and not of outward influence. Pastor William didn't doubt that God had intervened in Jacob's life, but everything surrounding this particular revelation seemed to be contrary to what the pastor had come to expect. Yet that's exactly why Pastor William couldn't shake the feeling that this was not only God's doing, but that it may very well have far greater meaning than what he had initially anticipated.

"If this is not for himself, then who is God trying to speak to?" Pastor William quietly contemplated to himself.

The divine interaction between God and Man; the Creator and His children, laid as the foundation of Pastor William's initial interest in understanding God's influence in people's lives. An interest that would often arise an eagerness in the pastor's mind to learn and discuss the innate intricacies of God's intervention. Yet, for the first time in his life he was left disappointed at the end of such a discussion; to be left with more questions than answers, and a lingering uncertainty surrounding the very nature of Jacob's story.

The questions in the pastor's mind began to change as he meditated on the latter half of his conversation with Jacob. The request that Pastor William use Jacob's story to speak to those in need, those struggling as Jacob himself had struggled. Up until that day Pastor William had no idea of the difficulties that Jacob faced. The brief retelling of Jacob's childhood had already revealed far more to Pastor William than he had initially known. Dwelling on his own lack of insight into the lives of his congregation, Pastor William began to question how exactly he was supposed to reach out to those who, like Jacob, may be struggling in silence.

Pastor William started to recall the frequent altar calls he gave to his church at the end of each weekly service. An open invitation of prayer for those who were struggling with sin, temptation, emotional distress and burdens they could not bear on their own. More often than not, the invitation was met with a small, albeit genuine response from the church. However, despite the few that would come forward, there was always a sense in the back of Pastor William's mind that there were many who remained seated, internally denying their own need for prayer.

Growing up in the church himself, Pastor William was all too familiar with the excuses and justifications that people would use to reassure their choice to remain seated. The belief that they would be judged for coming forward. The continual denial of their own struggles, or believing their own prayers would suffice; negating the necessity of the prayers of those around them. Even the unwillingness to admit vulnerability and actually seek help in their times of trouble caused this lack of response.

Regardless as to the reason for their silence, Pastor William began to think of those who, like Jacob, had also remained silent about the inner struggles they were facing. How their unwillingness to accept the pastor's outstretched hand inadvertently limited the extent of his reach. Though he found he's congregation's limited response disappointing, the desire to help others remained in the pastor's heart. He soon began to wonder if the request Jacob had brought forth would finally allow him to reach those who would otherwise remain silent.

These thoughts and questions occupied Pastor William's mind for the duration of his drive back home. A trip that would normally feel brief, one he had taken countless times before, felt much longer than he remembered. The sun was still setting across the deep orange sky as Pastor William pulled into his driveway. The pastor parked his car before removing his keys from the ignition and reaching over to grab the papers still sitting in the passenger's seat beside him. After slowly climbing out of his car, he began to make his way across the aged and cracked walkway towards the front of his home.

  Stepping in front of the door, Pastor William reached out for the handle and pressed down on the lever, removing the latch from the frame before letting himself into his home. As he walked into the house he was greeted with the ambient sound of a radio playing classical music in the background. Something Pastor William's wife, Grace, habitually allowed to play, regardless as to whether or not the home was occupied.

  The familiar sound of soft violin and piano music which Pastor William had become rather accustomed to filled the otherwise empty house. A house the pastor and his wife had purchased just prior to their wedding. One they had bought with the intentions of raising a family, unfortunately despite their efforts and Grace's ambition, they had remained the sole residents of their home for the entirety of their lives. The music continued to play in the empty background as Pastor William placed his keys onto a small hook affixed to the wall before making his way up a short staircase and towards his study at the end of the hallway.

The door to his study was partially open, revealing a disorganized and unkempt desk covered with liturgical books and sermon notes. Grace was not fond of the messy state of her husband's study, but despite her efforts and continual reminders, it remained in constant disarray. Upon entering into his study, Pastor William pulled out a chair from its place in front of the desk before sitting down and switching on the lamp resting atop the surface of his work space.

Directly in front of the pastor, sitting atop the pile of notes rested a letter of particular importance. A letter of inquiry written from a younger couple, who Pastor William only had a vague familiarity with, seeking him to be the ordained minister to officiate their wedding. It was a tremendous honour which he was eager to accept, yet his focus had been divided during the days leading up to his meeting with Jacob.

After clearing some of the disorganized mess from the surface of his desk, Pastor William placed Jacob's papers in front of him once more before flipping through the pages to find the point at which he had left off.

*

As the years went by the lives of my family, friends, and myself continued to change, yet remained the same. Each consecutive year of my education would have felt like an ever repeating cycle of frustration if not for the comfort and support I received from those closest to me. Despite growing older the difficulties that I faced during the early stages of my education remained ever present. This was not simply due to a lack of effort on my part. Richard, Amy, Michael and Julia provided me with the encouragement to genuinely strive to reach towards some semblance of success, yet my efforts always seemed to be for naught.

Eventually my friends and I soon outgrew the only school the four of us had ever known. The time would soon come when we were to graduate and transition into our local high school. A new and unfamiliar environment; one I entered with cautious optimism, hoping I would find the means to overcome the mental block that plagued the former half of my education. Unbeknownst to me I was walking into an environment that only further pushed me down a path of emotional strain, and eventually led me down a dark path of depression.

As my education progressed, it quickly became apparent that the artistic subjects that I had deeply resonated with, had been pushed to the side for the sake of more structured and methodical courses. Subjects like mathematics and science that rewarded formula memorization over creative thinking and natural inspiration. Those were the courses I struggled with the most, yet they were the only ones that apparently had any relevance in the real world, or so I was led to believe.

Despite the apparent lack of importance the artistic courses had on my overall education, I still managed to find an emotional escape in the form of the empty backdrop of an open canvas. A plane for me to lose myself in; a world in which I was the author and creator, the god of my own reality. Any lingering feelings of emotional strain or depression that I had become accustomed to completely vanished in the midst of my own creativity. The freedom that I so desperately longed for became a reality as I forged a landscape of my own desire.

These were the moments I longed to remain in, the moments that gave me relief from the harsh realities of my existence. It felt as though time ceased to exist every moment I delved into another blank world. Unfortunately, the hours continued to pass as the world around me remained unchanged. As much as I wanted to linger in my own creations, separated from the emotional strain that I continually prayed for release of, the lives of myself and those around me continued to move forward.

Much to my reluctance, the time would come when I had to shift my attention away from my artistic endeavours and towards the subjects that were given priority in my academic future. My focus was often divided, but I forced my own diligence to better my academic standing; and yet my efforts bore no fruit. I would often barely find myself passing above the threshold of failure, but I was never able to reach the same heights as the rest of my peers.

We all seemed to be running the same race, jumping over the same hurdles, despite my attempts to remain on par with my peers, I always felt as though I was falling behind. I was tirelessly sprinting to catch up, only to see others effortlessly outpace me. Despite the encouragement and support I received, it always felt as though I was destined to remain at the end of the pack. My exhausting struggles soon birthed a deep seated feeling of emotional strain and distress, a feeling rooted in the belief that I was of lesser competence than my closest friends and family.

The emotional frustration remained

shackled to me as my friends and I continued through our education. We progressed through the grade system together, yet not necessarily as a cohesive group. With each year our classes and classmates changed, relationships and bonds formed and faded over the course of our adolescence. Despite the continual changes throughout our youth, the friendships between Richard, Michael, Amy and I remained steadfast through it all. The time we spent together was as enjoyable as it had always been, but as time passed certain feelings between us began to develop.

The relationships I had with my friends began to deepen over the years, but it was clear that the relationships between some of my friends deepened more than others. The childhood friendship shared between Michael and Amy began to evolve into a youthful affection. It became clear to the four of us where Michael and Amy's relationship was heading. However, despite the evolution of their feelings, the bond we shared and the friendships we cherished remained ever present, unchanged by the new relationship forming between two of my closest friends.

The excitement we all felt at the developing relationship was soon coupled with an unwarranted feeling looming in my heart. A feeling I despised, yet one I couldn't ignore. As Michael and Amy's feelings for one another continued to deepen, I began to notice an internal and unspoken feeling of jealousy growing within me. A jealousy that was almost overpowered by the happiness that I felt for the both of them, yet one that remained nonetheless.

My jealousy was not rooted in any affection I felt towards Amy, but of a natural yearning to have the same companionship I saw developing between two of my closest friends. While I knew that I was not alone in such a desire, I continually believed that the companionship I sought after would remain beyond my grasp. The genuine support I showed my friends masked a feeling that I wanted to abandon, one that I wanted to be absolved of. During those moments of emotional distress I continually sought God's wisdom and intervention; both for the companionship I yearned for as well as release from my own emotions. I remained in prayer, faithfully awaiting God's answer, but received only silence in response.

I often wondered if Richard harboured the same feeling of childish jealousy that occupied my mind. Richard's more theatrical and outlandish personality seemed to convey a feeling opposite to my own, yet in the back of my mind, I couldn't help but question whether or not he was using his personality as a means to cover how he truly felt. Being the most outspoken one in our group, Richard was often the most vocal of his support of Michael and Amy's relationship. However, outward expressions of support can frequently act as a facade to hide internal feelings that would never see the light of day. A facade I was well acquainted with.

I was unsure if there was any validity to the thoughts I had of Richard's feelings towards Michael and Amy's relationship. It may have simply been wishful thinking on my part, a means for me to feel as though my jealousy was justified. Perhaps I felt that if someone else were to share my unwanted feeling of envy then I would be absolved of the guilt that I felt by harbouring such feelings in the first place. I knew that wishing one of my closest friends to feel a shared sense of jealousy, one that I prayed for release of, was wrong. Despite knowing this, my frustration would often cloud my own rationale.

In spite of the unwanted jealousy in my mind, I was supportive of and happy for Michael and Amy nonetheless. They were still my friends, and I wanted what was best for them. Over the course of our adolescence we all began to mature and grow, yet we all remained the same people at our core. Michael was still the same friend we all looked up to; the one who seemed to have the maturity and wisdom of someone far older than himself. We all admired him, and it quickly became apparent as to why Amy had initially developed an interest in him. It wasn't long before Amy's initial interest became a mutual feeling of affection shared between the two of them.

Regardless as to how Michael's relationship with Amy was developing, he wanted all of us to remain friends. Our childhood friendship was something that we all deeply cherished and Michael refused to allow it to fade away simply for the sake of forming a deeper relationship with Amy. As time passed we began to change as people, but our friendship was something that we held on to. It was our relationships that provided me with a single refuge in an encroaching storm of emotional strain. A refuge that provided me with solace in the midst of what was an overwhelming battle of frustration and depression overtaking my mind.

It felt as though there was an insurmountable block within my mind, one that felt as immovable as it did impenetrable. An eternally prevalent obstacle that remained present despite my prayers to God for wisdom and understanding; prayers for Him to bless me in the areas that I continually struggled with. I recited the same prayers day after day, week after week, waiting with faith that God would answer my cries, alas, I was left bereft of a response.

In the midst of God's silence I began to witness those around me continually and effortlessly achieve the success that I so often strove for. Seeing their success didn't give me an initial reason for frustration or jealousy, but instead provided a genuine desire in me to reach my own academic achievements. I wanted to feel as though I was equal to them, as though I was as competent as them, but with each attempt I fell short.

I desperately wished the feeling of falling behind those around me only existed in the confines of my school, yet it remained and perpetually grew outside of those walls. For every step that my friends took ahead of me, Julia took two. Every achievement I strove for, she effortlessly attained. The contrast between Julia and myself would have otherwise dragged me further into the depths of depression, if not for the continual emotional support she provided me.

The frequent encouragement I often received from my friends and family instilled in me the slightest shred of optimism, in what otherwise felt like a bleak environment. I wanted to believe there was an untapped potential that existed within me, the same potential I was once led to believe existed within everyone. I wanted to believe that Richard, Michael, Amy and Julia saw something inside of me that caused them to believe that I could achieve the same levels of success that they had already met. However, I felt as if I was only disappointing them, as though they continually placed their expectations upon me, only for me to fall short time and time again.

I knew that wasn't the case. I knew that the expectations they had of me weren't comparable to the unrealistic expectations I put upon myself. However, it was a mentality that I couldn't seem to abandon. The unending thoughts that I was continually coming short of their expectations seemed to repeat in my mind. An unending mental tic that I could never seem to ignore, regardless of the lack of validity of those very thoughts.

The emotional strain and distress that I had experienced throughout my education slowly transitioned into a slow spiral into the depths of depression. The unchanging mental block that prevented me from understanding my teachers fed into my frustration and ultimately depression, which, in turn, caused my mental block to seem even more insurmountable, which further fed into my depression. In my mind I was drowning. I had nowhere run. Nowhere to turn to. All that I had to hold onto was my relationship with my friends. They were the ones who kept me afloat in what felt like an endless sea of despair.

During those bleak moments I continually prayed to God for a breakthrough. Seeking divine intervention amidst an ever receding faith that He was truly listening. 'Faith to move mountains', a belief I held onto, trusting that God would shatter the insurmountable mental block in my mind. However, despite my faith, I found myself reciting the same daily prayers up until the last day of my education.

To perpetually suffer from depression and mental frustration, one I had continually sought God for deliverance of, only to have it plague me until the final ring of the school bell was disheartening. The logic as to why God would allow me to experience such a difficult time in school despite my endless prayers was something I couldn't comprehend or understand. Beyond seeking a breakthrough I was continually seeking understanding as to why God would allow me to endure such difficulties without providing me relief or restitution.

'God, why didn't You intervene? Why didn't You help me? Why won't You release me from my depression?' Such questions have echoed throughout all of history. Questions rooted in the same genuine and honest curiosity that exists in the minds of children, inquiries that had served as a crossroads for

so many people on their spiritual walks through life. As was the case with my prayers, those questions continually remained unanswered. The culmination of such questions and the emotional distress and depression I wrestled with for so long would soon elicit a different feeling entirely.

For so long I felt as though God had abandoned me, cast aside for the sake of so many others. That feeling of abandonment slowly evolved into the beginnings of resentment and anger. To feel anger towards a God that I was told loved me and cared for me beyond comprehension felt unjustifiable. Yet everything I had experienced up until that point felt contrary to what was supposed to be the very nature of God Himself.

As my education concluded I would soon embark on a new journey in life. What I had initially believed to be the light at the end of an otherwise desolate tunnel, only led me into what felt like a barren wasteland. The depression that I hoped to be rid of would eventually begin to crescendo as all our lives moved on, due to both my own decisions as well as for reasons that were beyond my control.

4

After Richard, Michael, Amy, and I finished our formal education we inevitably began to go our separate ways. Our friendship remained intact, yet our differing paths prevented us from seeing each other as frequently as we had grown accustomed to. We all had our own lives to figure out, our own ambitions and dreams to follow. While growing up we all had dreams of the lives and careers that we wanted; to be rich and famous, to be able to achieve the limitless potential that we all were told was hidden within each of us.

As we grew up our ambitions became

more realistic and attainable. Dreams of becoming famous and changing the world slowly transitioned into desires to follow a more traditional lifestyle. All those around me began to decide on what careers to pursue while I remained uncertain about what path I desired to follow. The uncertainty I was experiencing wasn't exclusive to myself, however. So many of my peers remained at a similar crossroads, and yet I appeared to be the only one without aim. While those around me seemingly had a myriad of interests or passion to pursue, I remained standing at the sidelines, struggling to find a viable path to follow.

My initial interest and apparent skill in the arts seemed to be the most logical step, but finding a means for me to even begin following such a career path was easier said than done. 'Starving artist' was a title I was already well acquainted with. To be told, albeit indirectly, that my only apparent ability was something that wasn't even worth pursuing was beyond discouraging.

As the years of my youth reached their conclusion, I began to feel an obligation from my parents and teachers to find a path that would lead to a stable and secure future. Feeling forced to pursue a career or further an education that I had no interest or passion in pursuing felt daunting. The growing pressure to find a career path only fed into an overwhelming feeling of anxiety towards an uncertain and ambiguous future.

Contrasted to my own uncertainty, Richard, Michael and Amy always seemed to have their lives relatively planned out, or at least, more focused than my own. Amy's path always seemed to be the most obvious of the four of us. Her natural motherly tenancies gradually developed into an interest in working with children, more specifically, teaching. This interest slowly began to grow into a deep passion. I couldn't deny her ability to teach, it was often due to her efforts and tutelage that I managed to graduate alongside her, Richard and Michael.

Both Michael and Richard had their own goals and careers which they had already set their mind on during our years in high school. Richard, the more theatrical and colourful of the four of us decided on a path that didn't initially feel as though it was well suited to him. One that felt as though it confined his natural talents, yet in reality it was one that allowed him to embrace the outlandish personality we had all come to know.

For so long we had always believed Richard's personality to be one of performance and theatrics. The eccentric creativity he expressed was in actuality a window into the colourful imagery that existed within his mind. Richard wanted to develop the skills to properly convey his thoughts into something tangible; a story. A career that on the surface felt so limiting to his natural talents, yet in reality it was one that gave him the most freedom. To be able to create a world rich with characters and cultures, and to truly give life to the imaginative world that we all knew had existed in his mind since we were children.

Michael's path was the most ambitious and difficult of us all. Like Amy, Michael had a desire to help others. The wisdom and moral compass he naturally had as a child continually developed as he grew older. He had always possessed a vague idea as to the kind of career he wanted to pursue, yet he was always so uncertain about what profession he truly desired.

As the years went by the realization of what Michael wanted to make of himself began to dawn on him. He longed to find a career that allowed him to follow what he believed to be morally right, a means for him to use his own natural wisdom and judgment for the sake of others. He decided to undertake the long and arduous journey of working towards becoming a judge. He knew that an education and career in the area of law would place a burden upon himself and his relationship with Amy, yet it was one that he fully embraced, despite being aware of the daunting challenge that was looming just beyond his sights.

As history repeated itself, I once again found myself struggling at the end of our metaphorical race. I witnessed those around me striving towards the careers and professions they wanted to pursue while I was still without focus, without clear direction; entirely uncertain of what I was to do with myself. In my uncertainty I sought those closest to me for wisdom and direction as to what my next steps could potentially be.

I was provided with a vast range of answers, yet I remained as uncertain about my future as I had always been. All the answers I was given felt empty, or at least shallow. I was often given very typical responses that one would expect; follow my passions, learn a trade, go to college for a post-secondary education that would only work as a means for me to simply postpone the situation I was currently facing.

As I reflected upon the myriad of potential opportunities that laid before me, I sought a particular path above all else. Beyond the answers I was given, I desired to know God's will and path for my life. I continually prayed, day after day, desiring the Lord to speak into my life. However, the answer I was given seemed to be the opposite of what I was anticipating, opposite of what I had once believed to be the means for God to speak into someone's life.

During my time as an adolescent in my church, I was taught about hearing the word of God; listening and discerning the unmistakable voice of the Lord. For so long I sought God for His wisdom and understanding in the intricate plan He had supposedly laid out for me. Though many Christians sought God's direction, so few are truly blessed with a revelation. It seemed that every one of my prayers was left unanswered. I felt entirely ignored, and understandably so. Revelation and discernment of God's will was something that I yearned for. Yet at the moment when God finally began to speak to me, the moment at which His voice had finally become distinguishable among the chaos that continually perpetuated my mind, I was at an absolute loss.

Often we expect, or at least hope, that God would bless us with a discernible answer to our prayers, a clear and concise understanding of His plan for our lives. This is a desire that so many people before me have held, yet despite my faith, when God actually began to speak I was left with more questions than answers. With each path or potential opportunity I brought forward to God I was left with an answer, but without direction. During every prayer I felt an overwhelming sense from God that I was deliberately, albeit unintentionally, praying against His will for my life.

It felt as though God was continually advising me away from every possibility that I considered. Even in the area that I considered to be my one and only talent, a skill that I had always believed that God Himself had blessed me with. Still I felt the unmistakable presence of God deterring me away from actually utilizing it. 'Why would God bless me with a natural skill, yet direct me away from pursuing a career using my artistic abilities?' It was a question that I continually proposed to God, and yet, much to my expectation I was only met with silence.

The dwindling optimism towards my future and the undeniable feeling that God was directing me away from every available opportunity felt disheartening. The seeds of resentment and anger towards God began to grow as I lingered behind my peers, trying in vain to find the direction that they found so effortlessly.

During that time I watched the lives of my friends and family continue to move forward while I remained standing at the sidelines, awaiting an opportunity to walk alongside them. Despite my steadfast desires to join them, I felt as if my life had become stagnant. It was a bittersweet feeling witnessing those closest to me take the next steps in their lives. The excitement shared among us as Richard, Michael and Amy embarked on new journeys in life was coupled together with a sorrow that the one solace I had in my life, my one and only refuge was slowly moving beyond my grasp. The sea of despair I frequently found myself drowning in soon evolved into an overwhelming storm of helplessness. A storm that instilled a sense of isolation, and further dragged me into the depths of depression.

It wasn't long before Richard, Michael and Amy left their childhood homes to pursue their passions, but in seeing their departure, I began to notice a feeling of loneliness welling within my heart. A sense of melancholy that the bond I shared with my closest friends had reached its conclusion. Though the distance between the four of us hindered our relationship, we all swore to remain in contact with one another. Through technology we could hold onto the friendships that the four of us so deeply cherished.

However as our lives steadily began to change, we struggled to abide by our initial plan to remain in contact with each other on a regular basis. The constant conversation between us eventually devolved into simple updates on our lives. Richard, Michael and Amy continually provided insight into the journeys they had all embarked upon, and yet I had nothing to offer on my end. My friends were aware of my struggles, and would at times provide me with the encouragement I desperately needed during some of my bleaker moments. However, despite their supportive words and my own efforts, I still faced tremendous difficulty finding the path that God had supposedly designed for my life.

While my friends were aware of my current employment situation, or lack thereof, they were entirely ignorant of the perpetual feeling of loneliness that had manifested itself since their departure. It was an isolating solitude, one that was understandable given the circumstances, but still persisted regardless of the contact I kept with my friends. As our lives continued to progress, the unavoidable reality that I would be forced to find my own path became an overgrowing weight upon my shoulders. Eventually, the pressure of life began to take its toll on me and I was forced to seek out whatever opportunity I could find.

I decided against going back to school to further my education. Memories of the anxiety I had endured while struggling to overcome the mental block during my initial education was enough to reject the notion of entering the school system once again. The knowledge that I would be there alone, away from my friends, away from the only solace that kept my sanity only further solidified my decision to pursue another path.

Without an education to gain I decided to seek out employment. During these moments God continued to speak to me. I sought after potential opportunities, and yet there was an unmistakable feeling that God was directing me away from my selected paths. I was caught in the middle of two choices; either I continue to wait for God to reveal the direction He was calling me to, or I submit to the pressures of life, forcing me to move forward, with or without God's direction. I knew that I had to make a choice and despite the overwhelming feeling that I was deliberately defying God's direction, I still chose the latter. It would only be after I relinquished my faith that God would answer that I would begin to understand why He was calling me to have patience in His timing.

I was limited in the amount of opportunities that I was able to apply for. With no educational achievement other than a high school diploma and no training or workplace experience to speak of, I had to rely on nepotism to provide me with my first stint of employment. My first foray into the workforce was given to me by my father, a welder and fabricator by trade.

I had some semblance of knowledge of the trade due to the numerous times my father would discuss his work while I was growing up, but actually setting foot into his field was different than I had initially anticipated. Only after seeing the environment with my own eyes was I able to fully understand the vocation my father had pursued. Through my father's efforts I soon began to undertake the long and arduous task of becoming an apprentice. Despite the incredible opportunity that laid before me, there was an ever-growing feeling of anxiety that I was going against God's purpose for my life. It felt as though with every step towards this new career, I was inadvertently taking a step away from God.

Given my lack of ability and experience in the area of welding and fabrication I was nothing more than a second pair of hands; a gofer for the more experienced tradesmen. As I became more accustomed to the practises of the industry I was soon given the opportunity to learn the trade firsthand. I was taught the basics of welding, fitting and fabrication; the use of various tools and machinery, as well as basic interpretation of drawings and blueprints. Over the course of my apprenticeship I became rather competent at the art and skill of welding. Yet, despite my growing ability, there was an unmistakable sense of hesitation that persisted in my heart each day I remained working.

There was no doubt in my mind that God was calling me away from the path that I was pursuing, away from the opportunity I was given. I would often pray into these feelings, continuing to seek God's wisdom, and yet the only answer I could discern was that His will for my life differed from the one I had chosen. A perpetual sense of hesitation and uncertainty lingered in my mind each day I remained welding; one that would feed into the anxiety that still remained within the depths of my mind. An anxiety not necessarily for my own future, but instead for my life itself, as though God was answering my prayers, but remaining silent all the same.

In spite of how I felt I knew that I had to focus on any semblance of optimism I could manage to find during that period of time in my life. The faint lights at the end of the tunnel gave me hope beyond my own nearsighted perspective of my life. There was reassurance in knowing that I would be laying down what could very well be the foundation of my life through the skills I was developing and the money I was earning as an apprentice welder.

Despite feeling that God was directing me away from the path I was going down, for the first time in my life I felt as though there was a path that I could see and one which I could actually follow. Despite the growing weariness that I felt in my heart and mind, the knowledge that I could finally walk alongside my friends and family provided me with a feeling of hope towards my future that I had never experienced before.

This was a feeling that seemed so foreign to me. The optimism that now existed in me, no matter how faint, seemed to drive away much of the anxiety that had lingered since my time in school. The uncertainty that brewed in my mind when contemplating my future became at ease when I began to focus on the newly visible path. I wanted to continue to pursue this new career in spite of God's direction, but as I trekked further down this opportunity for my life, God began to speak louder, eventually the feeling of optimism evolved into something very different, something unlike anything that I had previously experienced.

A feeling much darker than I could have ever anticipated soon arose; an emotional manifestation of nihilism. Any sense of optimism that once existed in me eventually began to fade away, just as the faint light of a dying candle will eventually be consumed and overtaken by darkness. Even my faith, the foundation of my life, was dissipating. I began to doubt the belief that I once firmly held onto; the belief that God truly had a purpose for my life. I started to question how God could have a plan for my life if He Himself refused to give any indication that His own plan even existed.

It quickly began to dawn on me that the anxiety and growing nihilism I felt was the repercussion of me indirectly, although in a sense quite literally, walking away from God. I had knowingly turned my back on the direction that He had given me. The faith that God was present in my life, the faith that I held onto despite the depression I had endured during my education, had entirely disappeared, leaving behind a nihilism greater and darker than anything I had known.

I didn't know where to turn to. I knew that I couldn't continue to live a life like this; one plagued by an ongoing battle with my own sanity. The thought that I would be able to hold onto the small shreds of optimism amidst the storm of nihilism I was enduring was facetious. I understood that in order for me to follow the path God had for my life I had to remove myself from the environment that had initially caused my separation from Him. However despite that understanding, I knew that by leaving my current profession I would be abandoning a genuine opportunity for me to provide myself with a stable future. These doubts continued to perpetuate my mind despite knowing that if I were to separate myself from God, then I doubt that it would be a future I would want to live in.

However, I was given my apprenticeship through the efforts of my father and the generosity of his employer, and I couldn't help but feel as though if I were to leave I'd appear as ungrateful or unappreciative of the opportunity that was given to me. Almost as a habitual response I prayed for an answer. Whether what happened next was as an answer to my prayers, or just unfortunate timing on my part, God began to move. He provided me the opportunity I had sought after; the means for me to step away from the path I had chosen without offending my father or my employer, but one that had come at a cost greater than I could have ever imagined, and heavier than I could endure.

*

The startling sound of the front door shutting awoke Pastor William from his engagement in Jacob's story. Grace, Pastor William's wife had finally arrived home after her day out of the house. While stretching his out his hunched-over back, Pastor William turned his head towards the window of his study. To his surprise, the darkness of night had been cast over the world outside of his home.

During the brief moment he spent gazing out of the window, the creaking of stairs underneath Grace's feet could be heard as she ascended the steps to the second floor of their home. Walking past her husband's study she glanced inside to see him staring out the window, still sitting in front of the pile of papers resting atop his desk.

"Still haven't found the time to clean up, have you?" Grace remarked. Pastor William turned to her and smiled guiltily, "I suppose not".

"Perhaps in the morning you'll find time to organize yourself. I'll be turning in soon, you're welcome to join me whenever you're ready." Grace said as she gently closed the door.

Pastor William smiled softly as he heard his wife walking towards their bedroom. He slowly began to flip through the pages of the story again before he grabbed a black bookmark from among the clutter and placed it atop the page he had left off before closing the booklet. He reached across the pile of papers and turned off his desk lamp. The light of the room immediately dissipated as the pastor stood up. He stepped away from his desk and began to make his way towards his bedroom where his wife was waiting for him.

The house was silent as Pastor William

laid awake in bed. The thoughts of Jacob's story and speculations of the revelation to come prevented him from falling asleep. The unseen battles and emotional conflict that went on inside of Jacob's mind was something that he was entirely unaware of.

      As the pastor of a church, he was well acquainted with the variety of humanistic struggles those of the church had endured both in the present day and throughout the course of history; depression, anxiety, loneliness, abandonment, and loss of faith. These were the trials that so many people of the church struggled with on a regular basis. Pastor William himself was well accustomed to those feelings, however it was the feeling of losing faith that seemed to resonate most with the pastor.

      Despite eventually becoming the leader of his church, prior to earning the title of 'Pastor', William had often wrestled with his faith and belief in God's presence and purpose. The notion that all Christian's had a blind faith was something he found shallow and unfulfilling. He often found his own faith to be an ongoing struggle, but one that he fully embraced. During his younger years William had believed that by questioning the Bible he was gaining a deeper insight into the word of God, and that by simply accepting the Bible at face value he would be denying himself of greater revelation and understanding of God's divine nature.

Despite the pure intentions of gaining greater insight into God and the Bible, William became aware that as he further questioned God, he became more doubting of his own faith. The philosophical arguments of theodicy and ethics that echoed throughout history become much more convincing over time. As he further delved into those ideas, William felt himself slowly separating from God. The nihilism which Jacob had described was something that William was all too familiar with. The prevalence of his nihilism would eventually evolve into pessimism. An increasingly depressing view of the world, one that had encapsulated any shred of hope and optimism in the young man's life; yet one that had become the very foundation of his faith.

Looking on the world through the dark lens of nihilism, William saw those around him, his peers and neighbours, living lives that seemed to be filled with a joy that was almost entirely absent from his own life. This direct contrast to his own life caused William to look upon others with an undeserved sense of disdain. He believed their joy to be out of ignorance of the dark realities of the world around them, yet in truth it was the very opposite.

Their joy wasn't rooted in ignorance of

the cruel realities of the world, but in their willingness to focus on the light amidst the prevailing darkness. This was a perspective contrarian to William's outlook, the same outlook that had dragged him further into the depths of nihilism. He was unable to rationalize how someone could acknowledge the darkness of the world, yet remain hopeful all the same.

He had begun to wonder if there was something he had missed; an area in which he may have lacked understanding, or was misinformed of the nature of the world and of God. The same fervour to question the Bible which led William to separate himself from God, soon brought him back to the question of theodicy, how both evil and good could simultaneously exist. The question of why a good God would allow such a dark world to exist was the foundation of William's nihilism, yet in his own reflection, he began to realize how such a contradictory idea could actually be true.

Just as darkness was the absence of light, evil was simply the absence of good. The more William pondered on this revelation the more he began to understand why he so often felt nihilistic. The negativity and darkness that consumed his emotional reality existed as a result of his separation from God. Upon reaching such a conclusion William began to reflect upon his own life, and the time leading up to that very moment. The all consuming negativity that he found himself living in originated from the moment when he started to lose his faith in God. As the one light that existed in his soul had been snuffed out, darkness naturally began to take over, and he realized that his own negativity was in essence his own doing.

He wanted to be free. He wanted the light to cast out the darkness that existed within his heart and mind. He began to seek out God and His word once more, yet this time it wasn't out of questioning and doubting God, instead it was about rediscovering and rebuilding his relationship with his Heavenly Father. The agnostic lens in which he read the Bible and viewed the world around him was replaced with a genuine desire to understand the true depths of God and His divine nature.

As months passed, the depth of William's faith deepened from where it had even been prior to his mind succumbing to the darkness. He began to believe that everything that had happened; from his early stages of faith, to his fall into nihilism, and ultimately his return to the Lord, was all by God's design. A path that William believed he needed to walk in order to secure his previously pliable faith.

He accepted all of this as 'God's will';

an absolute and unchanging design and plan from God Himself. William began to believe that God's will for someone's life was absolute and his own free will was simply an illusion. This was a mentality that William firmly held onto for much of his life. The notion of God's absolute will became as much a foundation of William's life as it was a comfort, something he could rely on in times of distress.

In William's eyes God's will was an anchor that provided him with a sense of peace in times that would naturally cause feelings of unrest and uncertainty. He believed that every decision, every choice was predestined by God, and as a result he had no control over his own life. His belief provided him with an unyielding and uncompromising faith in God, while absolving him of any and all guilt for his actions. For since he believed that his actions were beyond his control, wrongdoings were not of his discretion.

As the night progressed the thoughts running through Pastor William's mind eventually came to an end as he finally began to fall asleep. Hours passed before the light of the sun eventually shone across the horizon and began to flood into the master bedroom of Pastor William and Grace's home. The natural light illuminated the room and eventually roused Pastor William from his slumber. He awoke and turned over to a rather familiar sight; Grace, still sleeping peacefully next to him. He wanted to take advantage of the still morning and return to his study to pick up where he had left off in Jacob's story.

    The pastor carefully rose from his bed, trying his best not to wake his wife from her slumber, before quietly walking across their room towards the hall and into his study. The pile of papers remained on his still cluttered desk, resting exactly where he had last left them. The protruding black bookmark still in place among the pages, indicating where the pastor had last left off. He pulled out the chair from its place in front of the desk, sat down and began to flip through the papers until he eventually came to the bookmark. He shifted himself further into his desk and began to delve once more into Jacob's story.

5

*

For so long my struggle was one that I kept hidden from those around me. My family and friends were completely oblivious to the emotional storm that existed in my mind. However, I knew of one other person whose life was far more difficult than my own. A life that they were forced to live, yet one they seemed to be completely and blissfully ignorant of. While my life was one of emotional and mental distress, theirs was of physical and mental limitations; and unbeknownst to me, one that would eventually become the catalyst to my revelation.

Despite the creeping nihilism within

my mind, and the mental unrest I had become accustomed to, there existed an aspect of my life that would fuel envy in the eyes of another. The knowledge that there are those who, despite having monetary and earthly success, would be willing to abandon their own possessions for the sake of longevity. It was a humbling perspective that provided me with a gratefulness for my life, amidst the darkness dwelling inside of me. The appreciation for my health was reinforced through the continual reminder of what I routinely saw within the walls of my home; my younger brother, Alexander.

Ever since the day Alexander was born he was reliant on those around him. While this was to be expected as an infant, Alexander's necessity to have a constant caregiver remained throughout his childhood and thereafter. The true nature of his health concerns had always eluded me in my youth. I was initially led to believe that was how God had made Alexander. However, that very notion would eventually give rise to the question of why God would allow someone that He apparently loved beyond comprehension, to have a life that was so limited compared to the rest of my family.

As I grew older I eventually learned that Alexander's condition was due to a severe case of cerebral palsy, one which would develop into more serious health complications. The rest of my family simply accepted Alexander's condition as being 'God's will', an acceptance I found upsetting at times. I couldn't help but feel as though it was a means for my family to find comfort and reason in the reality of my younger brother's life. This was a reality they didn't want to accept, yet one they had to live with nonetheless. The burden of caring for Alexander, a child who was unable to comprehend his own existence, understandably placed a tremendous deal of stress on all of us. His well-being was a responsibility we had all accepted, yet drove us to our peak of exhaustion.

Alexander's life was a double-edged sword. He was unable to experience the aspects of adolescence we all take for granted; riding bicycles, building friendships and developing a sense independence and self-reliance. Yet at the same time it seemed as if he was unaware of the seemingly endless despair that plagued humanity and the world around him. The latter was an indirect blessing in disguise, at least it was from my own nihilistic view of the world. Jealousy wasn't the right word to describe how I felt. To be envious of someone in his condition would be foolish, but to see someone who would live their entire life without having to experience the dread of depression, felt at times almost favourable to my own situation.

My parents, Julia and myself all wanted to be able to help Alexander, yet everything seemed beyond our control. For so long I felt as though it was my duty to protect him. Not due to his condition, but simply due to the fact that he was my younger brother. Similar to how Julia seemed to have an unspoken understanding of my life, and showed her support to me through my own struggles, I couldn't help but feel as though it was my responsibility to show that same care for Alexander, regardless as to whether or not he truly grasped the situation.

It seemed that no matter where I turned to; from my education, to my apprenticeship, to my own family, I couldn't escape the melancholic realities of the world around me. Eventually the already weakening foundation of my life would begin to break down as Alexander's dimly lit life began to fade away at an unprecedented rate. In addition to, or possibly due to his tragic health complications, Alexander's condition quickly escalated, eventually causing my family's greatest fear to become a reality.

More urgent medical care was necessary as Alexander's health began to wane. The familiar layout of the home he was raised in was suddenly changed as he was brought into the cold and sterile environment of our local hospital. As the unforeseen consequences of Alexander's condition became more severe, the unwanted realization as to what was to come began to loom over my family. Despite having the means to visit my brother during his final days in the hospital, I rarely took advantage of the opportunity. To this day I'm uncertain whether or not I truly regret those decisions. Despite the love I felt for my younger brother, I couldn't bear to have my last memories of him be lying in a hospital bed, clinging to life. Seeing Alexander in the hospital may have been the appropriate thing to do, however the inescapable reality of what was to come became a greater deterrent and would eventually win over the choices I made.

  My once warm and welcoming home gradually became a house devoid of happiness as the days went on. The unspoken reality of what we were all enduring was almost tangible, almost as though the depression I internally battled had broken out of my mind and began to manifest itself within the walls of my house. It felt as though the rest of my family had been lost within the sea of despair that I had become almost accustomed to. There was no escape we could find amidst our emotional distress. Despite the comfort my family had in trusting Alexander's life in

God's hands, they were still desperate to find a way to break free from the inescapable reality which we were all stranded in.

The sombreness of our situation began to affect us in different ways. My parents seemed to be the most affected among the four of us. Ever since Alexander's birth my parents had devoted much of their time and energy into caring for him, attempting to provide him with a comfortable life despite his circumstances. Yet, as they saw their youngest child, the one who they continually prayed for, lying in the hospital, begrudgingly aware of the inevitable outcome, they felt as though all their efforts were in vain. It seemed as if God was refusing to make himself known in that situation, causing my parents to stumble in an area they so desperately wanted to remain steadfast.

The foundation of faith that my family's life was built upon began to waver in their hearts, a feeling which I was all too familiar with. Through my parent's eyes it felt as if God had turned His back on their earnest and genuine cries. Their faith, while not entirely shattered, began to falter, almost though it was directly connected to Alexander's life. For each day Alexander remained on Earth, each day his life remained on the brink of extinguishing, their faith diminished further.

Julia's reaction to Alexander's

situation felt contrary to her usual expressive personality. Her response seemed to be the most minimal and sombre of us all. The once bright and optimistic older sister that I had known seemed to become quieter as time went on. Her reaction wasn't an outburst of tears, or a flood of grief that is commonly experienced amid such dark circumstances. Instead, Julia remained silent; a stillness that began to quiet the optimism that she had previously radiated. I believe Julia had always been aware of the darker possibilities for Alexander's life, and that the optimism that she so often seemed to portray masked a facade of her innermost fears and concerns for her youngest brother.

Despite it all, my own emotional and mental state seemed to be the same. The feeling of depression and despair that my family was enduring was something that I had learned to live with, a pain that I had felt for so long that it seemed as though it was a part of me. Yet, only now did I feel as though I was able to truly convey and express exactly what I was internally experiencing. Alexander's situation was as much a catalyst for me to express my own emotional struggles as it was a means for me to truly realize just how accustomed I had become to the feeling of depression. It was in that moment that I could finally see for the first time what I was battling with internally.

The bleak outlook that I continually felt had been actualized before my eyes. It was a sombre awakening to be able to finally see just how far down the hole of depression I had fallen. The direct contrast that I noticed in my parents and sister; to see their lives and personalities change so drastically from the people I had known them to be was shocking. Witnessing them devolve from their typical demeanour while my own emotional state remained unchanged provided me with a much deeper understanding as to the extent of the darkness which I had been living in.

Everything began to change as time went on. Any optimism that my family desperately clung to slowly began to fade with each passing day. Though the frequency which my family would visit the hospital gradually increased, my mother remained by Alexander's bedside for almost the entirety of his admission, only returning home to briefly recuperate from the bleak environment of my brother's hospital room. Perhaps it was her motherly instinct to continue to care for Alexander despite his circumstances, or it could simply be due to her wanting to remain by his side during the limited time Alexander had with us. The rest of my family would join her from time to time, yet it was apparent that the next time she would be stepping through the doors of our home she'd be missing a part of her that could never be restored or replaced.

As a result of my mother's stay in the hospital, my father remained at home with Julia and myself, the full responsibility of supporting our household had been placed on his shoulders in my mother's absence. The time my father spent at home was often preoccupied with prayer or scripture. I was uncertain if he was trying to find comfort in the word of God, or if he was attempting to discover a validation or understanding as to why God would allow his youngest son to slowly die right before his eyes.

Occasionally my father would leave his Bible open on the table in our living room; an aged copy, one he had used for as long as I could remember. The translation he read was the King James Bible, one full of small notes written on the sides of the pages, underlined verses, bound within a cover that had been slowly worn down over the years. While seeing his Bible open wasn't an anomaly, I began to notice that during that moment in our lives, my father remained on rather specific books; Job, Lamentations and Ecclesiastes. Books focused on the dark realities of human nature, documenting Biblical narratives into depression and loss.

My father was well accustomed to the

written word of God, yet during that moment in our lives he remained focused on Biblical stories that reflected his own sense of hopelessness. Perhaps it was an effort to better understand the pain he was going through and to find the strength he needed during that time. The account of Job documented a man who remained steadfast in his faith despite God permitting the removal of his tremendous blessings. 'The Lord gave, and the Lord hath taken away', an old verse that I believe gave my father the strength to hold onto the last remaining ounce of faith that he had left during that point in our lives.

My father often spent his devotional time in silence and solitude. Perhaps it was a means for him to remove all the unwanted distractions from around him, allowing him to focus on God alone. Yet it was during this moment in our lives when he became far more vocal with his prayer, possibly as a means to figuratively and literally fill our house with God's word and presence. As the days drew on, my father's devotional time continually increased. It appeared as though the more time my father spent in prayer correlated with his own desperate desire for God to listen to his cries.

He and the rest of my family were not alone in our prayers. Our burden and pain was something we bore ourselves, yet there was a supporting foundation beneath us the entire time. Much of our church's congregation, or at least those who were aware of our circumstances, were increasingly vocal of their prayers for Alexander and the rest of my family. People from all walks of life, those who had dealt with comparable situations, offered their support for us, yet in spite of having a large church family surrounding us and caring for us, we felt as though we were entirely alone.

Their prayers and concerns were certainly appreciated, yet it was something that I continually felt was unfulfilling. There was no question that people were genuine about their prayers for us, but I often doubted that God would actually provide an answer. After all, why would He only listen once the rest of my church prayed while initially ignoring the prayers from myself and my family?

My family hoped and prayed for a miracle; a work of divine intervention that would then strengthen the faith of our church and of myself. A supernatural act of healing that would allow us to know that God was truly present in our situation. A sign that He was willing and able to show us his supposed unending love by rescuing Alexander from his own physical prison. We prayed tirelessly and ceaselessly, seeking and crying out to God with expectant faith that He would answer. But above all else, we prayed for God's will be done at that moment in our lives.

We desperately wanted God's will to be aligned with our own desires, an act of submission and faith that I know many others have continuously prayed for. We were willing to lay down our desires for God's intended plan for Alexander's life. We understood that His will may, in reality, be the exact opposite of our prayers. However, there was an underlying belief that God's will and His plan for our lives was greater than our own desires, and we were to have faith in His discretion for our lives. We all prayed, yet the day still came, the day which our darkest fears became actualized, and completely changed my perspective of God, and my outlook on life.

The rain poured down upon our roof that afternoon. Dark clouds covered the sky almost signifying a premonition of what was to come. We were all fearfully anticipating each day for the past two weeks. Every time we received a phone call or text notification we held our breath in a nervous apprehension as to what we would potentially hear. Each time felt as though we were one step closer towards the inevitable reality that we were all dreading.

My father, Julia and I sat together in our living room. Whether that was a coincidence or not was something I still wrestle with from time to time. The rain continued to pour as the concern in our hearts grew. Eventually the silence was broken by a sudden ring of my father's phone. It was a sound we had all heard countless times before, yet this was different. There was something unsettling about it. My father, Julia and I all seemed to have an almost clairvoyant understanding of what we were about to hear, as though the ringing of the phone itself signified the news we all anxiously feared.

My father's phone conversation was brief. Julia and I remained silent during that time, unable to hear what was being said on the other side of my father's phone, while still having a complete grasp as to what my father was hearing. After repeating "Yes" and "Okay" over and over, my father eventually hung up his phone before slowly placing it on his lap. Following a brief pause my father sank his head into his hands and began to silently weep for his lost son.

Julia looked over to me, her eyes quickly filling with tears. She was unsure about what to do or what to say in that moment; completely at a loss, as we all were. I simply sat there, trying to process exactly what was happening. I had anticipated how I would react in the days leading up to that moment; I thought I would be overcome with sorrow and grief, or scream and cry, and yet when the time had finally arrived, I remained silent.

Our home was quiet for the remainder of that day. The continual rain pelting against the window provided the only ambient sound in an otherwise silent house. There was nothing we could do at that moment in time. We were all caught up in the shock we had tried to brace ourselves for, yet when the time actually arrived we were entirely caught off guard. Time had seemingly slowed to a crawl before we lost track of it completely. The sound of a key unlocking the deadbolt on our front door broke the silence and brought our attention back to the world around us.

My mother walked though our front door and made her way to the living room where my father, Julia and I had been sitting for what had felt like an eternity. We all turned to her. Tears were running down her face as she looked upon us. She closed her eyes and shook her head 'no', before walking up the stairs towards my parents bedroom. The closing of my parent's bedroom door echoed down the stairs before the silence overtook our house once again.

6

The silence lingered within the walls of our home for far longer than any of us had anticipated. We prepared for a difficult recovery process, one filled with grief and sorrow, but it wasn't until we had lost Alexander that we began to comprehend the pain we would soon endure. It wasn't just the loss of his life that seemed to affect me, but the fact that he had to endure a life full of unwarranted limitations. Alexander was the most innocent among us, he didn't deserve such a life or untimely fate, yet the tragic realities of our world were entirely impartial.
    Day after day we waited and prayed

for relief from our emotional strife, for God to give us peace and comfort in our time of pain. We were continually told that Alexander was in a better place, and there was a faint reassurance in the belief that we would one day see him again in the perfect presence of God. We all desperately clung to whatever semblance of hope and comfort that was offered, yet there was nothing that could truly relieve us of our sorrow. The old adage that time heals all wounds felt like a delusion, one that we desperately wanted to be true, but in reality felt like nothing short of false optimism; a lie that one day we would be absolved of our own emotions. This wasn't a simple injury, or feeling of heartbreak. This was the loss of someone near and dear to us, someone that we loved and cared for, and someone who had left this world forever.

For years I was desperate to find an escape from the depression that consumed my life. To be free from the mental unrest that plagued my mind was something I had ceaselessly prayed for. Whether it was a cruel joke or reasoning beyond my own understanding, God released me from my own pain and anguish, but at a cost far greater than I could bear. My grief had all but silenced my depression, but brought forth an emotional turmoil beyond anything I had previously experienced. The grief lingering within me felt isolating, yet I knew it was felt by the rest of my family as well.

The loss of Alexander shook the foundation of my family, and our faith, to its core. It began to feel as though God had removed Himself from our lives. Despite the feeling of nihilism that had been consuming my life during the previous year, I remained believing that God was still present in our lives due to the faith the rest of my family held. The faith I saw in my parents and Julia began to fade during the weeks following Alexander's death. I wanted to remain in faith, I wanted to continue to believe that there was a meaning behind all of this. Alas, I was struggling to rationalize why a loving God would allow such a travesty to happen.

Each member of my family experienced and dealt with the grief in a different way. Julia's naturally bubbly and jovial attitude began to dissipate. The optimism that she once emitted became overshadowed by a sorrow that seemed to overtake her heart and mind. A sorrow not rooted in depression, or fuelled by anger towards God, but as a result of her reluctant acceptance of the reality she found herself in. I soon began to realize the pain Julia was experiencing was far greater than I could have ever expected. While I was unfortunately accustomed to a dark feeling of depression,

Julia had become accustomed to a life that always appeared much easier than my own. The unspoken depression and frustration that Julia could see in me was something she understood, but I don't believe she had truly experienced it for herself until that day.

While Julia's life became grey, my father became distant. The Bible my father had worn out as a result of his endless searching within God's word eventually became covered by a faint, albeit ever growing layer of dust. The faith he so firmly held onto remained in his life, but had transformed from a foundation and into a lifeline. It became a thread he held onto in hopes of finding justification and understanding as to why he had lost his second son. As time passed he became more despondent. He desperately clung to the thin lifeline of faith, but it became clear that the once strong foundation of his life was slowly dwindling into a remnant of what it once was. All that remained of his faith was the slightest optimism that he would one day meet his son again in Heaven.

Despite how Julia and my father had changed, it was my mother who seemed to have the most impactful feeling of loss and grief, but one that was the least noticeable in contrast to the rest of my family. Outwardly she appeared to be the same woman. There were no traces of sorrow in her personality, no sign of despair in her composure. There was simply silence; an expressionless, emotionless silence. An unspoken acceptance that there was nothing that could be said or done to bring back her lost son.

Despite her outward appearance, there was no doubt in my mind she was enduring the same heart wrenching pain we were all experiencing. My mother's steadfast demeanour, one held in lieu of our family's circumstances emphasized to myself and the rest of my family just how much of a toll Alexander's passing had taken on her. While one would expect a mother to wail or sob uncontrollably at the loss of her son, the unspoken acceptance my mother expressed was all the more powerful in spite of its silence.

In the days and weeks following Alexander's death I spent a majority of my time dwelling in the isolation of my bedroom, unable to find the means or strength to return to the life I once had. Given the tragedy that my family had experienced I was allowed a leave of absence from my apprenticeship. I received what initially felt like an answer to my prayers, as though God was providing me the means to leave the industry He was directing me away from. But in reality, it felt far more akin to a punishment than anything else.

I was absent from the distractions of the world around me. A separation that, in actuality, only caused me to be further consumed by my grief. The sea of depression that I found myself lost in would eventually evolve into an all-consuming whirlpool, one that seemed to pull me further and further down to the depths of an emotional and empty abyss.

In an effort to find solace during that time, I attempted to return to the one outlet that gave me a genuine feeling of purpose in spite of everything that I had dealt with during my adolescence. I wanted to return to the freedom that I found in my artistic abilities. There were a plethora of options available to me, yet I decided to turn to the one that felt the most accessible. I arose from the bed that I had found myself laying in during the majority of my days. Passing by my desk, I walked towards the window of my room. The closed blinds before me cast a comforting darkness that initially felt like cover for me to hide behind, a veil that protected me from the outside world. In reality it was a self-made prison, one that prevented me from truly facing my pain and allowing me to escape the abyss that I found myself sinking further into.

As I pulled the cord hanging from the right side of my window, the natural warm light of the sun instantly flooded into my bedroom and cast out the veil of darkness that I had become so accustomed to. I returned to my desk which was now bathed in the sun's illumination. Opening one of the draws to my left, I pulled out a small pile of papers and grabbed a handful of pencils before placing them atop the desk in front of me. I sat there, pencil firmly gripped in my hand, the tip of the lead resting on the blank paper. I had absolute freedom for my thoughts to be given form; a world of my own, a landscape for me to command, and yet there was nothing. My mind was rife with emotions, a proverbial storm which had often been the foundation of many great artworks in the past, yet it was one that left me bereft of any inspiration.

I sat there for what felt like hours. The outlet I had thought would provide me with an escape from my grief instead left me only to wallow in my sorrow. Whilst staring at the pages, my mind began to wander once again. I reflected upon not just Alexander's death, but everything that seemed to lead up to that moment, everything that I had lived though.

The depression I had endured, my struggles in faith, and the abandonment I felt whenever I sought after God for comfort or understanding. The memories of all that I had endured began to parade in my mind, and riled up a culmination of emotions as I reached my breaking point. The thoughts and emotions that festered in my mind began to unravel one by one. My built up frustrations added fuel to the firestorm that was consuming my sanity.

I wanted to be free. Free from my own emotional turmoil, to be released from this life that God had given me; for my existence to be erased from this tragic world. This was a feeling of despair that I'm certain many other people have experienced, and one that has unfortunately led some to take the irreversible step to permanently remove themselves from the Earth. It was a recurring thought that arose amid the darker moments of my life, and one that seemed more and more enticing as my life continued to move forward.

I couldn't bear it anymore. I placed the pencil down next to the pile of papers in front of me before standing up from my chair and walking towards the foot of my bed. I sat down on the edge of the mattress and I cradled my head in my hands. Tears began to run down my face and pooled into my palms. I sat there in silence, crying out to God in a final attempt for Him to actually reveal Himself to me, to give me reassurance that there was a reason for everything I had to live through, everything I had to endure. As I lingered in that moment, my sorrow quickly began to manifest itself into an overwhelming feeling of anger.

My teeth clenched as my anger grew. My hands trembled and my eyelids became tighter with each passing second. I began to quietly whisper to myself,

"Why? Why?"

The volume of my voice began to increase. My emotions piqued as I reached my breaking point.

"WHERE ARE YOU?!"

I yelled aloud, my head still pressed against my hands, the tears still running down my face. I remained there, sitting and waiting in silence for God to answer. As the seconds passed my anger and frustration began to subside. A sense of calmness began to overtake me as the overwhelming depression that I had become accustomed to seemed to melt from my mind. Almost as though my outburst had released the pent up emotions that had been brewing inside of me for so long. Everything felt unmistakably different, yet I couldn't comprehend why. For the first time I began to experience the peace I longed for. In that moment I spoke again, repeating the same question I had just asked. A question no longer rooted in emotion, but in a genuine desire and longing to truly know that God was there. To know that He would respond to my prayers, despite a lifetime of silence.

"Where are you?"

A few moments of silence passed. I remained sitting on the edge of my bed, my hands still covering my eyes.

"Here."

There was a voice, audible, yet without a distinguishable source. A voice unlike any I had heard before. One that was calming, yet commanding. Powerful, yet peaceful. I slowly lifted my head from my hands. My eyes remained closed despite no longer being covered by my palms. I took a deep breath before opening my eyes to a sight almost incomprehensible and unbelievable, yet tangible all the same.

*

Grace opened the door to her husband's study only to find him hunched over his desk, his eyes glued to the papers in front of him. Her gaze turned to the room around him, letting out a subtle *sigh* towards the untouched state of the room he had spent his entire morning occupying.

"Rather productive morning I take it?"

There was a slight cadence of sarcasm to her voice, masking the underlying irritation that Pastor William immediately recognized. Even in that brief moment, he could sense the slight annoyance that she exuded over his procrastination at organizing his work space.

He raised his eyes from the papers and began to look upon his desk before turning his attention to his wife standing within the door frame.

"I suppose not..." Pastor William said reluctantly.

Grace's attention shifted away from the state of the room and onto the papers that she had seen her husband reading late into the previous evening. It was a rare occurrence for Pastor William to be so enthralled at a story or paper for him to read it as frequently as she had seen. As far as she was aware, her husband had spent only a brief moment of time in bed next to her before returning to the papers before him. Grace was accustomed to the sight of her husband sitting at his unkempt desk while working on his weekly sermon. However, her curiosity began to pique as she inquired as to what had captured her husband's fascination.

"What is it that you've been reading?" Grace asked.

"Do you remember the Stame family?"

She paused for a moment.

"...Yes," the name arose memories of the family's lost son.

"This is something written by their midd-" Pastor William caught himself, "By their son Jacob; a supposed God given revelation. He told me he felt as though God was leading him to share his story with others, and in doing so, he felt it was appropriate to first share it with me."

"Interesting..."

Grace entered the room and walked towards her husband seated at his desk. She stood behind him, leaning over his shoulder whilst casually glancing over Jacob's story. The recount of Alexander's passing reinforced Grace's sadness. As she continued to read Jacob's writing, she became more intrigued as to the nature of Jacob's apparent revelation. Being a pastor's wife, Grace was well acquainted with God and the Bible. While she and her husband shared the same foundation of faith; their understanding of God's nature differed.

While Pastor William believed God's will was absolute and unchanging, Grace believed God's design for humanity was of freedom and choice; to know God, or live separated from His presence. Despite the disagreements in their interpretation of God's nature, both Pastor William and Grace managed to find unity in the understanding that neither of them completely grasped the unmatched complexity of God and His divinity.

After a few moments of the couple reading together in silence, Grace turned to her husband,

"Make sure you don't get too caught up in all of this, you still have other responsibilities to attend to."

"I know, I know," Pastor William said, nodding his head in reluctant agreement.

Grace turned towards the door and proceeded to walk out of the room, closing the door behind her as she left. The sound of her footsteps began to fade as she descended the stairs into the main floor of their home. Finding himself alone once again, Pastor William turned his attention back towards Jacob's story. Turning over the page he had just finished reading, the pastor was greeted to something unexpected. The paper before him was almost entirely blank, similar to the title page found at the front of the story, with a single yet defining difference.

In the middle of the page was a single word, one that would catch the attention of any Christian and many other religious practitioners in the world: *'Heaven'*. Pastor William raised his eyebrows in curiosity. The accounts of people who had supposedly experienced Heaven was something the pastor was well acquainted with. While Pastor William found an inherent fascination with stories recounting personal experiences of Heaven, there was always an underlying hesitation to accept the validity of such claims. Although Pastor William would never immediately cast off their stories as false or disingenuous, his doubt remained as a small remnant of his previous mentality of nihilism which he was unable to fully rid himself of.

    He stared at the word far longer than he had expected. The growing and unwanted feeling of doubt prevented him from continuing to read the story that had initially captured his intrigue. Pastor William remained sitting in contemplation, reflecting back to the conversation he'd had with Jacob the previous day. He recalled Jacob's own acceptance and admission that his experiences, while apparently divine in nature, seemed to be beyond his own belief. It was Jacob's humble confession of him not knowing the realities of his own experience that allowed the pastor to finally turn the page.

7

*

-Heaven-

I opened my eyes to an environment entirely unfamiliar to me. The room that I had isolated myself within was suddenly replaced with a picturesque meadow scenery that seemed to be straight out of a masterful painting. The seemingly endless plains and rolling hills of grass and trees eventually touched the deep blue sky, displaying an exquisitely beautiful landscape beyond anything I had ever known. The multitude of flowers and greenery sprouting out of the ground emitted a sense of life that was far greater than any garden or field I had ever seen.

The sky and meadows were covered by a warm light that shone upon every inch of the land, yet to my surprise, the sun itself was absent from the sky above. The light of the world existed in absence of a discernible source or origin. In spite of the sunless sky, the very essence of nature itself was on full display right in front of my eyes. I stood in absolute awe, wanting to take in the perfection before me, yet almost expecting to wake from this dream-like state. Moments passed in anticipation of my awakening, yet I remained there.

I stood within the middle of this vast and endless landscape, yet despite being in a location I was entirely unfamiliar with, I never felt as though I was lost or astray. However, despite finding myself in a situation that would normally elicit feelings of isolation and anxiety, I felt a sense of peace that I had never truly known before. It wasn't until that very moment that I began to realize that all the worries and anxieties, depression and dread that I had become accustomed to were entirely absent from my mind.

The peace and relief that I had so desperately prayed for had become actualized. The unmatched beauty surrounding me and the unprecedented calmness that I was experiencing drew my mind to a conclusion I couldn't deny, yet one I couldn't rationally accept either. In my contemplation I reflected upon the voice that had spoken to me in response to my outcry. The voice with no source, the one that was as mysterious as it was familiar. In spite of the present denial that I was trying to convince myself of, my mind arrived at the same unacceptable conclusion as before. I wanted to believe that what I was experiencing was real, yet the unending doubt remained shackled to my mind.

As I struggled to wrap my head around my current situation, I felt a warm but silent wind begin to blow. A calming summer breeze gently blew against my body, as though I was being directed further into the meadow. Just as a boat's sails are at the mercy of the wind, I too began to follow the direction in which I was being led. A calming reassurance came over me, despite lacking any clear destination as to where I was heading. Guided by the wind, I ventured further into the meadow, uncertain as to where I was going or what I was being led towards.

The scenery became more captivating with each step, as if the world itself was growing around me. The wind continued to blow, pushing past me and towards rolling hills in the near distance. The caress of the breeze caused the multitude of foliage and flowers to sway and dance as I neared, their movement mimicking the rolling waves of the ocean. The wind carried with it fragrant scents of the flowers from the distant hilltops surrounding me. The natural and unrecognizable aromas combined with the mesmerizing landscape further solidified the conclusion I continually tried to suppress, yet one I was unable to deny.

As I continued to traverse the breathtaking landscape, I began to hear the faint echo of a waterfall in the distance, far beyond my vision. The sound of rippling water seamlessly blended into the calming atmosphere, and piqued my curiosity for reasons beyond my understanding. I stood atop one of the many hills attempting to locate the source of the sound. The sight of a small stream flowing in the distance soon caught my attention. My eyes followed the direction of the water before finally locating its origin; a small waterfall. However, it wasn't the sight of the cascading water that stood out to me.

Next to the stream, directly underneath a faint rainbow formed by the waterfall's perpetual mist, sat a man. The sight of another person was unexpected, yet welcomed. Despite being in the distance, there was an unmistakable and inexplicable sense of peace emanating from Him. Though His back was turned to me, and while I was unable to see His expression, I couldn't help but feel as though He was welcoming me towards Him.

With each step towards the river, the wind which had initially directed me into the meadow began to fade. I felt as though I was nearing my destination, and in essence, the reason as to why exactly I was brought to such an incredible, beautiful world. I soon found myself walking alongside the edge of the river. The light of the sky shone upon the river as the light's reflection glistened and danced upon the surface of the flowing crystal clear water.

I was captivated by the shimmering light reflecting on the surface of the water, but directly in front of my eyes, underneath the surface were small fish swimming against the current, moving in a direction parallel to my own. The fish effortlessly swam within the stream, moving against the current of the water almost as though the water itself was completely still. As I continued to walk along the edge of the river, the gentle chirping of birds overhead became audible. My attention was turned towards the bright, yet sunless sky as small birds began to fly overhead. Much like the fish, they were flying towards the very same destination I was already walking to. I began to realize that I may not have been the only one who was drawn closer to the area, or to be more specific, The Man sitting quietly by the waterfall.

The mist of the waterfall began to

dampen my face as I drew closer to its source. The birds were perched upon the surrounding rocks and the fish had begun to pool together at the edge of the river as I neared The Man. Despite remaining virtually motionless, fixated on the flowing water in front of Him, I couldn't deny feeling as though The Man was welcoming me to sit by His side. I walked next to Him and faced the flowing river before finally sitting down.

I remained silent during that moment, trying to piece together everything I had just experienced. There were questions circling my mind, yet amid that moment in time, I felt as though I was to simply revel in the peace and tranquility of the natural beauty surrounding the two of us. Still facing the water, The Man began to speak. His voice was identical to the one I had heard in my mind, the one that answered my cry out to God.

"Beautiful, wouldn't you agree?"

"It is." I said, still trying to rationalize everything that was happening.
Moments of silence passed as The Man and I continued to gaze into the pool of water in front of us; focused on the fish pooled together at the edge of the river. Each fish was attentively fixated on The Man sitting beside me, just as a young child intently waits upon their parent.

"I understand the issues that have

been pressing upon your mind." The Man said, breaking the silence that lingered between us. "I know the answers you've been seeking and the questions that continue to linger within your thoughts. I know the understanding that you've sought and the distress you've endured. Despite what you may think or believe of Me, I know all that you've gone through, and I want you to understand the reason as to why your life felt so unjust."

A few seconds of silence passed before The Man stood up,

"Please come with Me." He said, offering His hand toward me.

I was suddenly raised to my feet as I grabbed onto His wrist. For the first time I was able to look upon The Man face-to-face. His appearance differed from what I had anticipated; He appeared to be in His early thirties, younger than my own father. His dark complexion contrasted a pair of deep blue eyes which seemed to gaze into the very depths of my heart and soul. He was adorned in a simple white robe, one reminiscent of the attire I had seen in modern interpretations of Biblical stories. In contrast to His foreign appearance there was a familiarity to His presence. He was a complete stranger, yet it felt as though we had known each other for some time.

He softly smiled at me before turning

around and walking further into the meadow. I began to follow, remaining a few steps behind Him, attempting to piece together the nature of who He truly was. My doubt and denial prevented me from accepting the tangible reality which existed before me.

I remained walking in silence, continuing to take in the breathtaking scenery that surrounded the two of us, while the endless questions paraded through my mind. I didn't know where to start. I wanted to understand everything that was happening at the moment. Beyond where I was, or who this Man was, I wanted to understand what he meant by; 'Despite what you may think or believe of Me, I know all that you've gone through'. Whether it was out of anticipation or divine understanding of my mind, The Man began to speak into the very questions that echoed through my head,

"You're struggling to make sense of it all. You are tirelessly trying to wrap your mind around everything, both at this moment and in the midst of your life back home. You've longed for answers to your questions about the world and about Me. The reasoning for the abandonment you've felt, and the faith you've never been able to truly relinquish."

"So, are You who I think You are?" I asked.

"I am." The Man responded

"So why exactly am I here?"

"You're here because you want to understand. You have so many questions, as so many like you do. Yet, you've never been satisfied with any of the answers I've given you."

"How could I be? For so long I never even felt like You were there, all I ever heard was silence. I prayed over and over, but You never answered."

"I understand why you feel that way, I really do. Having faith in a God you cannot see, faith in a plan that so often feels more akin to chaos than order is difficult. 'All discord, [is] harmony not understood', or so they say. Even now, I'm standing before you, conversing with you face-to-face, yet you're still unsure about whether or not what you're truly experiencing is real."

"Will You finally be able to tell me why my life felt so unfair? Is there really a reason why my prayers were never answered?"

"The answer to that question is both 'Yes' and 'No'." He answered.

"What do You mean by that?" I asked, a lilt of uncertainty arose in my voice.

"I want to provide you with the understanding that you've so desperately desired, yet it won't be directly from Me, at least not in the way you may have originally anticipated."

"So it won't be some sort of lecture or sermon?" I asked, uncertain what The Man was alluding to

"I'm afraid not. Given the reason you're standing in front of Me, I don't think a simple explanation would suffice. No, there's a better way for you to understand."

"What exactly do You have in mind?"

"You shall see soon enough," He alluded.

By the time our conversation had concluded, we were standing atop a hill overlooking the vast and endless landscape. My eyes widened as I took in the entirety of the breathtaking world beneath me. The view before me was nothing short of stunning, but in my moment of amazement The Man turned to me, desiring my attention.

"Sit down, please." The Man said, gesturing His hand towards the ground. *I complied and began to lower myself until I was comfortably resting atop the surface of the hill. The Man joined me, sitting directly across from me; face-to-face, eye-to-eye.*

"For so long you sought understanding of My plan for your life and the lives of those around you. Yet in doing so, you were trying to comprehend something simply beyond your own capacity. To attempt to fully realize the infinite complexity of a divine plan is impossible for anyone but the creator

themself. To understand My plan, you must first understand Me. The relationship you had with Me gave you some insight as to My nature, but to fully rationalize My very essence requires a revelation beyond limitation. The answers you seek cannot be revealed through a simple epiphany or realization, and that's not My intention for bringing you here. My intention is for you to experience something far greater than that. To see the world beyond your own vision, to see the world through My eyes."

I didn't know what to do at that moment, I didn't know what to say. I sat across from The Man who had apparently laid out the very plan for my life. The only one who could provide me with understanding of the life I had been given, and the reason for the depression I had endured and the loss I had experienced. And yet in the face of all of this, I remained silently sitting, waiting for The Man to speak once again.

"Please, close your eyes." The Man said to me.

I shut my eyes, sealing off my vision to the world around me. The Man was no longer visible, yet His presence remained. With my eyes closed, I soon felt His hand rest upon my left shoulder. He began to speak to me, His words were indecipherable, spoken in a

language which felt familiar, yet

indistinguishable all the same. It was a language reminiscent of the people who could apparently speak in tongues. I wanted to discern His prayers, but alas I remained bereft of the ability to comprehend such a language.

Suddenly, everything ended. The sound of The Man's voice, the feeling of His arm upon my shoulder, even the ground upon which I was sitting entirely disappeared. I opened my eyes, yet to my utter surprise nothing had changed. The darkness which my eyes had become accustomed to remained. My eyes were opened and yet I was unable to see. As I attempted to comprehend exactly what was happening I heard The Man's voice one again.

*

The pastor sat perplexed at what he was reading, his eyes resting at the bottom of the page. The imagery of Heaven and God that Jacob had written about was contrary to what he had expected. The description of a vast and unending meadow elicited a sense of doubt within Pastor William, the imagery contradicted the proverbial streets of gold he had read in the Book of Revelation. Even the supposed description of God as a young man, one who never specifically or directly claimed

or denied to be the Almighty began to cast a

veil of uncertainty onto the pastor's mind. The desire to read further into Jacob's revelation remained, but whether Jacob's encounter was a tangible experience of God's direct intervention, or instead a metaphorical vision, pressed upon his thoughts.

      The internal contemplation of Jacob's revelation brought Pastor William's attention away from the pages and back to reality. His vision shifted from the white pages resting upon his desk and began to move across the room before finally reaching the window situated to his right. The bright light of the mid-afternoon sun shone upon the world just outside of the pastor's window, replacing the early morning sunrise which he had witnessed prior to his initial dive into Jacob's story. Pastor William squinted his eyes, as his vision started to adjust to the natural light shining through the glass. He was entirely unaware of how much time had passed since he had first returned to the pages earlier that morning. He had neither a reference point to know when he had first entered his study, nor any indication as to the current time of day.

      Regardless of the time, he could feel his body, more specifically his back, beginning to cry out; a feeling which he had become well acquainted with in recent years. The stiffness he often experienced was an

indication that he had remained stationary,

hunched over his desk, for far too long. He knew better than to allow himself to reach such a point of discomfort, but all too often his dedication to God's word blinded him from his own physical well being. The pastor's frequent obliviousness to his physical state inevitably resulted in him enduring such a feeling far more frequently than he would have preferred.

    It was often during those moments he would find himself in need of a break, a temporary escape from both his physical aches as well as the isolating environment where he had spent the entirety of his morning. Pastor William placed the black bookmark laying next to his arm onto the page which he had left off at, a placeholder to indicate where the pastor had finished reading, despite leaving the booklet of papers open atop his desk. He then proceeded to slowly and stiffly arise from his chair, carefully stretching out his back before stepping out of the room his wife had exited seemingly moments ago, yet it was clear more time had passed than he had initially thought.

    Thoughts of Jacob's story were still fresh in Pastor William's mind as he descended the staircase of his house. The sound of classical music grew louder with each step towards the main floor. The soft sound of a harp reached Pastor William's ears as he

neared the front door of the house. His shoes

were paired together and placed neatly upon the floor mat, a small gesture by Grace in an effort to keep their home in order. He slipped on his shoes while simultaneously grabbing his keys from a hook which they were resting upon, before opening the front door and stepping out into the world.

The heat of the afternoon sun pressed upon the pastor as he began to make his way down the front walkway of his home. The empty driveway in front of his house indicated that Grace had left their home earlier that morning. A myriad of questions, both about and towards God paraded through his mind as he began to walk down the driveway and into the familiar scenery of his neighbourhood. The imagery of Jacob's conversing with God face-to-face both mystified and intrigued the pastor. To be given such an amazing and blessed opportunity of witnessing the Lord of all Creation manifested as a tangible being. The inherent desire of all Christians to witness the physical presence of God resided within Pastor William's heart, yet he continued to question the validity of Jacob's claim.

Lost within his own thoughts, Pastor William was entirely unaware of a rather familiar sight driving past him; Grace, who upon returning from her day out casually waved towards her husband. Her gesture was

seemingly ignored by Pastor William who

remained so focused on his internal dialogue during his walk, that he was entirely oblivious to the world surrounding him.

After driving past, Grace pulled up to her house and into the driveway before parking the car and making her way towards the door of the home. As she passed through the threshold of the doorway Grace was greeted to the same ambient music her husband had heard before leaving their home a few minutes prior. The soothing melody of a harp continued to resonate within the walls of the house, bringing with it an imagery that Grace often associated with the stringed instrument; scenes of angels basking in open meadows underneath a cloudless sky, traditional depictions of Heaven seen through the eyes of historical artists. This was an imagery that Grace accepted, but unbeknownst to her was contrary to her husband's interpretation of Heaven.

As Grace walked through her home, she ascended the stairs to her and her husband's bedroom. Nearing their bedroom Grace turned her attention towards the door to her husband's study that had been left ajar. Against her better judgment Grace was hopeful that her husband had finally and reluctantly heeded her advice to organize his work space, alas when she opened the door the

expectations she had of a disorganized mess

were unfortunately met.

Following a deep *sigh* Grace proceeded into the room with the intention of organizing the unkempt mess her husband had procrastinated about for so long. The booklet of papers resting atop the pastor's desk caught Grace's attention. She recalled the brief conversation she had shared with Pastor William about Jacob and his apparent divine revelation. Her intrigue slowly evolved into curiosity as she carefully flipped through the pages before returning to the one that was laid open when she had first entered the room.

Grace sat down in the chair in front of the desk and began to read through the pages of Jacob's writing. The description and imagery of Heaven further confirmed Grace's interpretation of how the afterlife would appear. As she skimmed through the pages leading up to Jacob's depiction of Heaven, the directions of his life and his family had grabbed her attention.

Much like her husband, Grace was familiar with the Stame family. The brief excerpts she read of Jacob's story shone a light into a life she was entirely ignorant of. As Grace continued to glance over the paragraphs, the sound of the front door opening and closing echoed through the house. The sudden break in the silence caught her attention, but her focus still remained fixated on Jacob's writing.

The sound of footsteps walking through the main floor of the house shortly followed the closing of the front door. The noise grew louder as the footsteps began to climb the stairs before finally reaching the landing of the top step. Grace turned her head towards the door to her left. In the middle of the door frame stood Pastor William, gently smiling at his wife. He walked towards the chair Grace was sitting in, reached over her shoulder, towards a small disorganized pile of various writing tools, before grabbing a white bookmark and handing it to her.

"You're welcome to read along if you would like." Pastor William said.

"Well, don't mind if I do," Grace said, accepting the bookmark from her husband's outstretched hand. She placed it underneath the cover page of the story, stood up from the chair, and proceeded to walk around her husband before making her way out of the room. Pastor William sat back down into his chair, the stiffness that perpetuated the discomfort in his back had been all but resolved throughout the course of his walk.

With his back rested and his thoughts at ease, Pastor William turned to the pages of the story still situated on his desk. He began to flip through the papers until he located the

black bookmark he had placed prior to

stepping outside. His eyes focused on the last sentence he had read before delving into Jacob's story once again.

8

*

"Very soon you'll receive the revelation and understanding you've long sought after." The Man said, His voice once again having no discernible source or origin

For a second time I had awoken to a sight completely foreign to me. Despite initially awakening in an unfamiliar location, I once again found myself in an environment entirely unrecognizable. There was no landscape, no sky, no meadow. All that seemed to exist was an abyss. A vast and empty void, one which I seemed to occupy, yet my own physical existence was absent. I attempted to speak, wanting to respond to the man's voice, but in absence of a physical body I lacked the means to audibly talk. My internal dialogue began to break the silence as I attempted to discern my current circumstances.

"Where am I? What's going on?" I thought to myself.

"Your questions will be answered in due time." The Man responded.

I was able to hear the man's voice once again. Not as an audible sound, but as a thought spoken directly into my mind. I began to think, not only to myself, but in an effort to speak to The Man once again.

"What am I supposed to do?" I question.

"Soon you shall know, but you must first have patience".

The Man began to speak once again, His words echoed to the very edges of the abyss. His language reminiscent of the one He recited when He had initially spoken over me in the meadow. As He spoke, a single light began to flicker in the distance. A faint light that pulsated in the otherwise endlessly dark void. As The Man concluded speaking, the light slowly began to fade back into the dark void from which it was born. I waited in anticipation of what was to come. The moments following were far greater than anything I could have ever imagined. A sight that was as mesmerizing as it was spectacular.

An explosion of colours and lights burst outward from the very same location where the faint and flickering light first shined. The dark void was soon filled with vibrant streaks of light travelling in all directions. The continually expanding lights bathed the furthest reaches of the void, stretching into the distance far beyond my vision. Reverberating sounds of comets and stars soon echoed past me, travelling through the ever expanding sea of lights.

The understanding of what I had just witnessed was as captivating as it was humbling. The unimaginable sight of the birth of existence would initially feel incomprehensible, and yet it was as glorious as it was tangible. The awesome and absolute power of an almighty and divine creator was on full display in front of me. A being who possessed the omnipotence to form a universe from speech was truly deserving of the titles of 'Lord' and 'God'.

In an instant the once empty abyss of boundless darkness had been transformed into a brightly illuminated cosmos of stars and galaxies. One again I found myself surrounded in mesmerizing beauty. Two separate landscapes, virtually opposite one another, yet phenomenally beautiful all the same. As the last remnants of the expanding cosmos moved outwards, a single ball slowly drew closer to me. One without form; entirely void, covered in the same darkness that once enveloped the eternal abyss from which it originated. As the ball continued to move towards me the sound of crashing waves began to emit from its surface. The words and imagery of a particular Biblical book began to fill my mind.

I remained fixated on the sphere of water floating before me, waiting in anticipation of what I was about to witness next, alas there was nothing. I began to think to myself, both to process everything that had taken place as well as an effort to talk to The Man who had just spoken this universe into existence.

"Is that how everything was created?"

"In essence; yes. However, the process of creation takes different forms; from the birth of a universe, to the forming of life. You must understand that the subtle changes taken during the initial steps of creation allow for an outcome vastly different than one may expect."

"And this is supposed to answer my questions and prayers?" I asked.

"Take heed of that which is before you, for that is where your answer will reside."

I remained fixated on the small ball of water, still uncertain of what was to become of it, or more specifically, what I was to do with it.

"I don't get it. How is water supposed to help me?"

"Just as I birthed the stars around us, you are to create and shape the world before you."

"What do You mean by world?"

"You had already begun to recall the account of creation in the Book of Genesis; the light and darkness, the sun and the stars, and the formless, empty world. The same sea of potential that existed for my own creation now exists before you.

"So what you're saying is that I'm basically God of this world?"

"Yes,"

"And how am I supposed to act as God?"

"Just as I spoke the cosmos into existence, you have absolute reign over the world before you. For only when you see the world through the eyes of its creator shall you gain the wisdom and understanding you seek."

As the reality of the situation began to set in, my questions surrounding the empty and desolate planet evolved into thoughts of creation. Within my hands I possessed the all encompassing and limitless power of God. With a single thought the waves on the surface of the world swayed and calmed. Storms *began and ended in an instant. Patterns of torrential downpours and perfectly still seas would alternate with each passing second.*

I continued to recall the accounts of creation as I commanded the waves of the sea. My recollection was not exclusively of the world before me, but of the stars and skies. With a single thought the stars aligned and repositioned. Patterns and consolations would form as a particular star and moon began to draw closer to the world. The sun's radiating light began to shine upon the surface of the water as the gravity of the moon directed the tides of the sea. The sun and the moon; light and darkness were now established, mimicking the beginnings of creation.

My focus shifted from the skies back towards the world itself. The waters remained still as thoughts and imagery of mountainous landscapes and deep valleys began for form within my mind. On my command solid ground began to rise from beneath the waves. The water began to move and separate as rising mountains and landmasses burst forth from the depths of the sea. Islands and continents began to form from the surface of the world before reaching their final resting place above the surface of the water. The emerging landscapes were empty and barren, completely devoid of any semblance of life; a world which was solely and entirely uninhabitable.

Plants and vegetation began to sprout forth from the ground. The once dry and infertile bedrock began to overflow with rich soil before finally birthing forth grass and foliage; transforming the once barren landscape into lush valleys and beautiful meadows. Trees and plants emerged from the planet's surface, flourishing into entire forests within a matter of seconds.

From deep valleys to dense jungles, from scorching deserts to frozen glaciers. The once empty and dark ball of water which existed before me not moments ago had evolved into a planet equal to that of the world which I called home. The heat of the sun began to warm the surface of the landscape, flowers and plants bloomed as lakes and oceans glistened in the reflection of the sun's light. Despite the natural beauty covering the world, the surface of the planet remained devoid of true life.

Mirroring God's own creation, my next step was clear; to form and spread life to the ends of the world. The knowledge that I would be giving life to countless individual creatures elicited an apprehension within me. The shaping of the world's landscape and geography was inconsequential compared to the task of creating sentience. I experienced a brief moment of hesitation, and yet within an instant, with a single thought, the entirety of the planet, both atop the surface and beneath the seas, were filled with life.

An abundance of life inhabited the planet; from the fish of the sea to the birds of the sky. The imagery portrayed within the beginning verses of the Book of Genesis had become actualized before me. During that moment, imagery of the Garden of Eden arose within my mind. The descriptions of a seemingly perfect paradise sequestered within a vast and barren world. Secluded within the garden was man; Adam, the provider and caretaker for God's creation.

The necessity for a person to tend to my world felt irrelevant, and yet, either through divine influence of the man, or my own understanding of my situation, I felt compelled to create my own 'Adam'. With my own authority I could create a world incorruptible by humanity's sin, the proverbial Heaven on Earth many dreamt of; the world God had intended for humanity since the beginning. By my own hands I could shape a world free from toil, free from the pain and emotional distress that I had become so accustomed to. And yet, the eternal question as to why God would allow His world to become rife with sin remained unanswered.

In that moment I had the means to ask The Man why He would allow humanity to fall so far from Him. The long sought after relationship I desired with God had finally been fulfilled, allowing me direct access to His limitless knowledge. And yet, I understood that my purpose for standing in God's position was not to seek His wisdom through conversation, but to witness the world through the lens of its author and creator.

I stood at the cusp of the final stages of my creation. I was given the perfect canvas, a world to be shaped and formed by my own thoughts. The absolute freedom that I continually sought after, the escapism that I desperately yearned for had become fully realized. I commanded the wind and the waves, I could speak mountains and deserts into existence, and soon I would create man to his fullest potential.

I gazed upon the planet and the life which existed within it. Until that moment, my account of creation mirrored that of God's written word, albeit with one single, important distinction; an individual with the capacity to live a life of purpose and meaning. Imagery of a world populated with people made in my own image began to form within my mind. My thoughts would eventually manifest themselves as living, breathing beings; men and women, young and old.

Mankind suddenly encompassed the world, but contrary to my expectations, they were lifeless, empty and stagnant. The contrast between the beasts of the world and that of humanity became suddenly apparent. Despite both possessing life, only the former of the two seemed to truly be alive. I commanded the absolute power to lay the very foundation of existence with a simple thought, but upon the creation of mankind, I seemingly lack the capabilities to manifest true life.

I meditated on the emptiness that existed within each person, attempting to understand why they were devoid of the very essence of life. Despite my omnipotence, I was left without an answer or explanation. I began to call out to The Man once more, seeking His wisdom in an effort to discern what my creations were lacking, and to determine how to instill their lives sentience and consciousness.

"What's happening?" I thought, both to myself and The Man, "The people are just standing there. Did I do something wrong?"

"Life is beyond simple creation," The Man said, "You have created the people and you have created a world for them to inhabit, that much is true. However, you are only seeing them from an outward perspective, and you only possess a surface level of understanding of the true depth of humanity. The wisdom and direction you seek resides within each individual man and woman."

"How am I supposed to figure out this 'wisdom and direction' if You won't tell me?"

"Look beyond the physical. Just as you are able to form the planet from your thoughts, man himself is a blank canvas, one for you to shape and mould by your own volition."

"If that's true, then why wasn't this necessary for the animals I created? They're both living creatures, why is it that humans are the only ones who are apparently missing life?"

"Both man and beast have the breath of life inside of them, but for you to understand the answer to the prayer you have been seeking, you must go beyond simply creating beings who are alive. You must understand that life is far more complex than what you may have once perceived it to be."

"I think I understand," I said reluctantly, *"I'll give it a try."*

My mind was full of doubt and confusion as I looked towards the people that I had created. The emotionless beings; stationary and stagnant. Beyond their physical and outward appearance I attempted to delve further into their hearts and souls. Through the lens of their creator I could see the depth The Man had referred to, one that existed within each and every human. The depth beyond their simple individual *personalities, but of life itself. Alas, despite peering into my creations' hearts and souls I became bewildered at what I had discovered. There was nothing, the external emptiness which I could perceive in each person mirrored an interior that was equally devoid of life.*

Parallel to my confusion, I began to feel a sense of familiarity in what I was witnessing. The emptiness that I could see within each person's heart and soul began to resonate with the memories I had of my life; the life that felt entirely devoid of God's presence. As I meditated on that thought, I was drawn towards a conclusion which would set the beginnings of my revelation into motion. The emptiness that I had observed within each person wasn't due to a lack of life, but instead it was a result of an absence of my plan, of my will, and of my presence in their lives.

My will was to create a world devoid of pain and hardship; to allow my creations the means to live the life I had long desired for myself. The perfect existence that myself and others yearned for, and yet God's apparent unwavering stand against such a reality resulted in a world overrun with sin. A desire in my heart to prevent such a life for those I had created began to grow. With a simple thought I could form my own world to be free from the curses that plagued humanity for the entirety of its existence. I could permanently erase the ceaseless pain and unnecessary loss that God allowed His children to endure.

My intentions were righteous and just. My intention was to shape a world free from sorrow and hurt, from depression and pain, from want and desire. I looked upon each person, each individual life. Every person housed a blank slate of limitless potential. The absolute freedom I had to instill my Will in the lives of my creations carried with it a seemingly insurmountable task; to forge an intricate and detailed plan for each and every person in the world. And yet, without a moment's hesitation I began to work.

I methodically laid the groundwork for each and every person's life simultaneously. The complexity to have billions of lives connected and interconnected would be impossible for anyone other than an absolute omnipotent being. I was conducting a symphony beyond comprehension, creating a plan so intricate and refined that the greatest minds of humanity could study it for a lifetime and not even scratch the surface of it's incredible depth. What initially felt like an impossible undertaking was achieved without the slightest bit of effort.

As suddenly as my work began, it was complete. The paths were laid and their lives were set. Satisfied with my efforts, I began to partake in the final step in God's original creation; rest. I took a moment to reflect upon the splendour of my work. The perfect world which innumerable people had prayed for throughout all of humanity's history had finally become actualized.

In my brief moment of Sabbath and reflection, the unforeseen consequences of my actions began to emerge. Despite my intentions, the emptiness that I had tried to erase from the lives of my creations was never truly removed, but instead became altered and magnified. I had initially thought that in creating such a perfect plan for everyone's lives I would be able to create Heaven within their world. However, the realities of my plan caused unforeseen and unexpected repercussions. The consequences of my actions inadvertently created a world opposite of my own desires, and ultimately created a reality that was as empty as the void from which it was birthed.

*

The perplexity that Pastor William initially experienced grew as he further delved into Jacob's aforementioned revelation. His questions began to accumulate with each successive page. The idea of Jacob establishing a plan for each persons' life greatly intrigued the pastor, as did the suggestion that such a concept had unintended and unwanted consequences. Despite becoming God, an omnipotent being of limitless potential, Jacob's attempt at manifesting perfection resulted in a world apparently devoid of the life he had instilled in his creations.

    As Pastor William continued to reflect upon the story before him, a sudden knock on the door of his study interrupted his train of thought. Grace stood on the other side of the door, attempting to pull her husband's attention away from the story and back into his own reality.

    "William, are you still in there?"

    "Don't worry Grace, I'm still here." he responded. The cadence of his voice acknowledging how much time he had spent secluded away in his room at the top of the stairs.

    "You've been cooped up here for a while now, would you fancy yourself a break?"

    "Perhaps a little later on," he answered. Pastor William turned his attention towards the window of the room; the light of the setting sun painted the sky a brilliant and vibrant orange. It was at that moment he realized just how much of the day had passed since he returned to Jacob's writing earlier that afternoon.

"Suit yourself, I'll be downstairs if you change your mind." Grace smirked, before returning back to the main floor of their house.

As the noise subsided and the silence returned, Pastor William's focus shifted back to Jacob's writing. He turned the page, revealing the next chapter of Jacob's account. A single word laid bare atop the white page, a word that resonated with the pastor, arising feelings of curiosity and uncertainty. A single word which had spawned an ever present debate within the spiritual and religious communities: *'Predestination'*. The very subject which had brought Pastor William out from his descent into nihilism and back into God's hands.

He felt a slight hesitation upon reading the word. The very notion that his understanding of God's design for humanity potentially led to the emptiness that Jacob had eluded to stirred within the pastor's heart. The apprehension Pastor William was experiencing was rooted in a subconscious feeling that Jacob had a very tenuous grasp of such a complex subject in comparison to his own understanding.

The pastor began to internally recall and recite arguments of predestination and free will as a means to further reinforce his unwavering belief in God's absolute and unchanging plan for his life. The pastor's reluctance subsided as he once again reflected upon the humbling understanding that Jacob's revelation wasn't intended to answer the unending questions surrounding God's nature and His divinity. Instead, it was a means to speak to those who've experience the same apparent injustice that Jacob had previously endured.

Pastor William used the brief lapse in his concentration to take a much needed break away from the pages he found himself lost within. He slowly began to stretch out his back and arms, his aching and aged muscles feeling a slight bit of strain since returning from his walk that afternoon.

He rotated his head to the analog clock mounted on the wall. Both of the clock arms pointed downward; the face of the clock read six-thirty. Knowing that he had spent the majority of his day situated in his chair, Pastor William declined pursuing the next section of Jacob's story, leaving the following page a lingering temptation for the morning. He picked up the bookmark which was resting parallel to the pile of papers before carefully placing it atop the nearly blank page. The black bookmark covered the only word written on the paper. Whether it was a coincidence or subconscious action on the pastor's part, the very mention of predestination was hidden from his sight.

    The pastor proceeded to close the bundle of papers, making sure both his and his wife's bookmarks were undisturbed from their place within the pages. He stared at the title written on the center of the first page; *'My Story'*. The eagerness Pastor William had felt when he initially heard of Jacob's first hand experience with God's divinity was devolving. The gradually developing unbelief within his heart and mind remained despite the pastor himself wanting to be able to accept Jacob's revelation as nothing short of God's divine intervention. Knowing Grace was patiently waiting for her husband, Pastor William raised himself up from the chair he had been resting in and began walking towards the door, leaving behind the papers which he would be returning to in the early dawn of the coming day.

    With the door now shut behind him, an effort on his own part to prevent himself from returning to his study in the night, Pastor William proceeded to walk down the stairs towards the main floor of his home. The smell of a freshly cooked roast began to waft from the kitchen up the staircase, meeting the pastor as he descended the steps. Grace was carefully placing down two plates of meat and vegetables just as her husband reached the landing. She turned to him, thankful to see that he had managed to pull himself away from the pages which had captured his attention since the previous day.

"So nice of you to join me." Grace quipped, warmly smiling to her husband.

'Thank you for waiting." Pastor William said, returning the same cadence and smile towards his wife.

"So tell me about this story so far." Grace implored as she sat down at the kitchen table. Her eagerness to know the story her husband had been reading had overtaken her patience.

"Very well," Pastor William responded.

Upon taking his seat Grace asked him to bless the food which she had prepared. The heat of the food radiated off of the plate and onto the pastor's face as he began to vocally speak a prayer over their meal. A typical prayer that was as much a vocal expression of thankfulness and blessing over the food, as it was a verbal habit the pastor would recite before eating. After concluding his prayer, Pastor William took a moment to enjoy the exquisite smell of the meal his wife had prepared before sharing a brief synopsis of Jacob's story thus far.

9

The conversation the pastor shared with his wife over their dinner gradually evolved into a philosophical discussion of God and His divinity. The differing viewpoints of God's nature held by the couple provided a cordial debate in trying to rationalize the meaning and purpose behind Jacob's revelation. The conversation eventually transitioned into the subject of theodicy. Both Pastor William and Grace attempted to dissect the rationale for why God would allow such pain and sin to exist within a world which He held absolute authority over.

The conflicting beliefs the pastor and

Grace held over the subject of God's design for humanity prevented them from reaching a sound conclusion by the time their dinner had ended. During the entirety of their discussion a single word remained burned into the pastor's mind; 'predestination'. The remainder of their evening was relatively uneventful. The air in the pastor's home was filled with idle conversation and banter one would expect between a couple who had been married for forty years. With their dinner concluded, the pastor and his wife cleared the table and began to wind down for the evening.

    The light of the sun faded as the darkness of night began to settle across the outside world, marking the end of another day. Grace excused herself from the kitchen just as Pastor William finished cleaning the remnants of their dinner. Shortly after putting the last of the dishes away, the pastor made his way to the living room of his house. Joining Grace, Pastor William sat down onto a large chesterfield facing the glowing illumination of a television screen.

    The imagery and voice of a news anchor welcoming his audience to the beginning of his segment projected into their living room. He began to recount world events from the past twenty-four hours, accounts of travesties and disasters routinely made headlines over the past few years, while economic and societal unrest remained the focal point of the daily news cycle. While Grace's attention remained fixated on the television screen, Pastor William's mind was still preoccupied with the conversation he and his wife had shared over their dinner.

    Fragments of the news stories began to trickle into Pastor William's thoughts as he continued to meditate on the subject of predestination. The persistent mysteries surrounding the logic and reasoning for natural disasters and travesties beyond human control stealthily crept into Pastor William's mind. Despite his own efforts to find purpose for such atrocities to exist, he only ever found himself reaching the same familiar conclusion that he refused to part with; the acceptance that God had full, unquestionable authority over the world. For it was His judgment of humanity's sin that brought upon the natural disasters much akin to the Biblical story of Noah.

    Yet, as he continued his contemplation, there was an unmistakable sense that he was accepting an answer that wasn't wise so much as it was easy. He was uncertain as to whether this was a result of Jacob's writing pressing upon his mind or God indirectly speaking into his situation. The sound of the news anchor's voice began to fade into white noise as Pastor William's focus gradually shifted away from the television and towards his own internal dialogue.

The unwavering acceptance that the pastor's life was fully and entirely controlled by God gave him a reassuring sense of faith in a world that was so consumed by chaos and pain. To accept everything as God's direction was an anchor in an unending storm. It was the foundation that his entire life was predicated upon, and for it to be challenged by someone who apparently received a divine revelation from God shook the pastor to his core.

His mind was torn for the remainder of the night. The desire to read further into Jacob's story persisted, despite the pastor's attempt to distance himself from his study until the morning. However, in spite of his own interest, the notion that Jacob was indirectly challenging the pastor's understanding of predestination arose a temptation in his heart to simply abandon the story altogether. The subconscious feeling of pride the pastor harboured subtly brought forward an undeserved, albeit faint feeling of resentment towards Jacob's revelation.

The uneasy feeling within the pastor's heart remained, despite his continual attempts to reaffirm his aforementioned beliefs. For the first time in his adult life, Pastor William's faith began to shake. It wasn't necessarily his faith in God that began to falter, but his faith in his understanding of the Bible.

A strong sense of doubt began to rise as he considered the possibility that he may be mistaken in his own interpretation of God's word. Either out of a natural instinct or a reaction to his own uncertainty, Pastor William began to pray. He sought after God's wisdom and reassurance in an effort to reinforce his faith and to be absolved of the feeling that he was misguided in his knowledge of God's divinity.

    Given his position as the head of his church, Pastor William was well acquainted with discerning God's voice from his own internal dialogue and interests. Although he had yet to experience the audible voice described in Jacob's writing, he was still capable of recognizing and interpreting the presence of God and that which He was speaking into his heart.

    The white noise emitting from the television remained in the background as Pastor William persistently prayed, waiting in anticipation for God's 'voice'. In spite of his expectations the only answer that Pastor William could discern amidst his own feelings of uncertainty was the singular word of 'patience'. He sat in bewilderment, God's answer to his prayers was not the clear direction he had anticipated, but to simply have faith that the answer would become apparent in time.

After begrudgingly accepting God's answer, Pastor William's focus was redirected towards the television. The anchor's speech and physical mannerisms indicated a rather bleak news cycle. Despite his professional demeanour, his voice began to lilt in accordance to the subject matter of his segment. He soon bid his audience a sombre farewell, one carrying with it a subtle wish for a more optimistic future in the coming days.

The credits began to scroll across the screen as Grace grabbed a remote atop the armrest to her right. She raised the remote towards the television before pressing down on the power button. Within a moment the light and sound of the television dissipated, leaving Grace and her husband alone in the silence of their living room.

Grace turned to her husband, his face displaying an expression of deep thought and reflection.

"What is the world coming to?" Grace rhetorically asked. Her question directed towards the ceaseless chaos, both natural and man-made that seemed to exist within every corner of the world.

"I just don't get it." Pastor William sighed, both as an answer to the question posed by his wife and in response to God's unsatisfying answer to his prayer. "I think I'll be retiring for the night." he said abruptly, the heavy thoughts still weighing upon his mind. He sought a quick end to the evening, a means to find rest from the confusion that consumed his thoughts, in addition to his dwindling interest in returning to Jacob's writing in the early morning.

"So soon?" Grace asked, surprised by her husband's wish to return to their bed so early in the night. "You've spent your entire day by yourself, reading that story. Even now, in the time I've spent with you this evening your mind has been elsewhere."

"I know, I know. Trust me, it's not my intention to be so preoccupied. It's just, I'm still trying to understand what's weighing on my mind. It all seems so improbable, but there's a truth to it that I can't really explain. Something about it feels so real. I don't know, maybe God will explain it to me later on."

"I'm still interested in reading it myself. Who knows, maybe I'll be able to figure it all out before you do." Grace joked.

"Oh, I wouldn't put it past you. You're definitely the smart one in this house." he teased.

Grace blushed at the complement, her cheeks and eyelids began to wrinkle as her smile quickly grew. Pastor William leaned towards his wife and softly kissed her cheek before standing up and bidding her goodnight.

"Enjoy the rest of your night. I love you." he said before turning around to begin his trek back to their bedroom.

"Love you too." Grace replied.

Then she lifted up the remote and pointed it towards the television once again as her husband left the room. Upon exiting, Pastor William walked towards the staircase leading to the second floor of his house. As he reached the summit of the stairs he proceeded to walk down the hall towards the master bedroom. A tinge of temptation began to fester in his mind, a faint desire to return to Jacob's writing. However, he internally acknowledged that if he were to dive back into the written revelation, he wouldn't be returning to his bedroom until the early hours of the morning, which would only serve to irritate his wife further.

Pastor William grabbed hold of the doorknob to the bedroom and twisted it. The metal hinges softly creaked as the door swung open, revealing a room entirely cloaked in the darkness of night. The scattered lights of stars sparkled through the window in the adjacent wall. Excerpts from the story arose within Pastor William's memory, feeding into the temptation he had denied himself of when he had turned his back to his study.

Upon entering the room the pastor

dragged his hands across the wall, blindly attempting to find the light switch in the darkened room. Despite having occupied the house for much of his life, he could never quite manage to remember the switch's placement in the dead of night. The switch seemed to always be out of reach, never exactly where he had last recalled it to be, despite remaining affixed in the same spot since he and Grace had first moved into their home forty years ago.

    Eventually his hand finally managed to ascertain its location. Within an instant the room was filled with a bright light, displaying a perfectly organized bedroom. The cleanliness of the room served as a clue as to where Grace had spent her time during the afternoon while Pastor William had remained secluded within his study. Closing the door behind him, the pastor proceeded to change into his sleeping attire before turning off the light switch he had so fervently tried to locate just moments ago.

    The darkness of night reappeared just as suddenly as it had vanished. Pastor William walked towards the bed in the middle of the room and lifted the blankets before crawling into the comfort of his bed. Lying awake, the pastor began to pray. It was a means to have the last moments of his day secluded in prayer with the Lord; a habit he had fallen into many years ago that quickly developed into a nightly ritual.

In addition to the typical prayers of thankfulness and reflection of the day that were expected of his final time with God, he also sought wisdom and discernment in deciphering the meaning behind Jacob's revelation. He desired for God to speak into his mind beyond a simple word of 'patience'. After audibly speaking his final "amen" the pastor turned his head over in an attempt to fall asleep.
Before shutting his eyes, his vision was once again fixated on the flickering lights shining in the night's sky just outside of his bedroom window. Recollections of verses in the Bible pertaining to the stars began to fill his mind, Biblical and mental distractions which slowly distanced the pastor from the state of sleep which he yearned for.

Despite his efforts to calm the restless thoughts from within his mind, the endless stream of questions regarding God's divinity continued to bombard the pastor's mind. Seconds turned into minutes. The silence and darkness in the room only served to further magnify his thoughts as the dark isolation prevented him from diverting his attention away from his own internal contemplation. The pastor laid in silence, entirely unaware of the length of time that had passed since he had first laid his head upon his pillow.

The unending train of thoughts within his mind were suddenly interrupted by the same familiar sound of the twisting doorknob and the creaking hinges the pastor himself had caused earlier. The sound of footsteps entered the room, yet the lights remained shut off. It was a courteous gesture by Grace to prevent her from interrupting her husband's sleep, entirely unaware her husband laid on their bed completely conscious.

The sound of Grace carefully moving around the room provided the pastor with the necessary distraction he required to separate his mind from the questions and imagery that perpetuated his wakefulness. Eventually the sound of Grace walking ceased as she made her way onto the bed. In the presence of his wife, Pastor William managed to quiet the distractions in his mind, allowing him to find the peace that would soon bring him to the state of sleep he longed for.

The night was still and the house was silent. The continual thoughts which buffeted Pastor William's mind had finally concluded. The internal struggle that roused within the confines of his mind had finally ceased as he laid asleep next to his wife. In his own ongoing effort to accept Jacob's revelation and discern God's answer to his prayers, the pastor's mind reached a point of exhaustion he rarely experienced.

    Dreams that would normally occupy a subconscious mind amidst its slumber were entirely absent from the pastor's sleep that night, as though his own subconscious had been put to rest. The stillness that existed in the walls of his home seemed to mimic the calmness within the pastor. The hours passed as the sun slowly crept towards the horizon, it's magnificent light poured onto the world outside of the pastor's home. As the sun continued to slowly rise, it's radiant light soon found itself cast into the pastor's bedroom, indicating the beginning of a new day.

    Pastor William awoke from his sleep and his unadjusted eyes were greeted by the bright light of the morning sun. Pastor William squinted his eyes while looking over towards Grace, still sound asleep next to him. He gradually gathered his energy, fighting off the lingering feelings of tiredness and fatigue that often accompanied his morning awakenings. He recalled the effort Grace had made the previous night of silently entering into the bedroom as not to disturb his 'sleep'. In an attempt to return the gesture Pastor William slowly arose from his bed, quietly walked towards the bedroom window, and carefully pulled over the curtains. The outpour of light was immediately cutoff as a faint darkness returned to the bedroom once more.

"Thank you." Grace muttered, much to her husband's surprise. He was unsure when his wife had awoken, but her words hinted at her desire to fall asleep once again. In an attempt to retain the quiet atmosphere that existed within the walls of their house, Pastor William exited the bedroom and returned to the adjacent room across the hall.

He stood in front of the door he had closed the previous night, an attempt he made to separate himself from the story that remained the focal point of his attention. The pastor grabbed onto the doorknob and began to rotate it. The latch soon disengaged from its place within the frame as the door opened for the first time since the previous evening. He stepped into the room, carefully closing the door behind him in an effort to prevent Grace from awakening yet again that morning.

As he walked into the room he placed his hands upon the back of the chair resting in front of his desk. He pulled it out from its place before stepping around and lowering himself into his seat. He sat at his desk, the pile of papers still situated on its surface, the two bookmarks still protruding from within the pages. He sat in silence, his heart and mind torn between his desire to accept Jacob's revelation, and to abandon it altogether. Pastor William placed his elbows onto the desk, interlocked his fingers, closed his eyes and began to pray.

"Lord, who are You? For so long I thought I understood Your nature. I thought I had grasped Your plan for my life. I have always believed that You intricately laid the foundations of my life and its direction. Yet, now I've begun to question everything. If Jacob's revelation is true, and his absolute plan for everyone's lives ushered forth unintended and negative consequences then did I always believe a lie?

"Did I blindly accept a false belief of predestination, when in reality it's the exact opposite? I just don't understand. What is the truth behind all of this? I know that Jacob himself acknowledged his own uncertainty, but I'm still struggling to truly accept it. God, I want to know, I want to understand. Please speak to me through Jacob's word. Bless me with the understanding that I'm lacking. Bless me with Your wisdom and understanding in this time, amen."

The pastor opened his eyes upon the conclusion of his prayer. The papers remained in place, entirely untouched since the previous night. Pastor William separated his interlocked fingers and began to run his right hand across the surface of the title page. As the tips of his fingers made their way to the tops of the pages, he touched Grace's white bookmark before eventually coming in contact with the black bookmark placed several pages deeper within the story.

His fingers pinched the tops of the papers, lifting them to reveal the page on which he had left off. Pastor William raised the bookmark from atop the page, revealing a white background with the single word that had struck a myriad of emotions into Pastor William's heart the previous day. The word that had never left his mind, and had arisen a storm of thoughts that persisted even after he had laid his head upon his pillow.

As he looked upon the word, a sense of calmness began to cover his body. The emotions that had manifested themselves the previous night had dissipated, virtually washed away from his heart and mind. The notion that God had eased his discomfort in response to his prayer was brought to the forefront of his mind.

The pride that Pastor William unknowingly harboured had been removed from his heart as the calmness continued to wash over him. With his emotions at peace, Pastor William turned the page over. His eyes briefly scanned over the words before finding their place at the top of the paper. He quickly found himself lost within Jacob's story; a revelation which would soon provide Pastor William himself with clarity in his own understanding of God's divinity.

10

*

-Predestination-

Before my eyes existed a world that appeared to be perfect in every regard; a world free from pain and sorrow, want and desire. Each and every individual, every being lived a life full of joy and peace, void of the sadness and depression myself and many others had endured. From my very thoughts I had created the world humanity had long sought after, a world brought to fruition not by the grace of God, but by the hand of someone born into a world full of suffering and turmoil.
The feelings of loneliness and abandonment ceased to exist within the confines of my reality. The often expressed

notion of "Heaven on Earth" had become fully actualized through an act of altruism by a being beset with the authority of God Himself. I began to meditate on the question of why such a reality didn't or couldn't exist within my own life? Despite seeing the world through God's eyes, I was unable to rationalize why God would allow those He apparently loved and cared for to experience such suffering. I was once again drawn to the only conclusion I could find; God either cared for a select few of His aforementioned children, or none at all.

"Why does pain and loss have to exist?" I asked, seeking The Man's wisdom and rationale for why such a question could even be asked in the first place.

The Man remained silent.

"I just don't get it. If I can create my own perfect world without effort, why couldn't I have lived in a world like this?"

Silence. An answer mirroring God's response to my lifetime of prayers. However, either through The Man's influence, or my growing instincts I felt as though His silence was not a result of His ignorance or uncertainty. Instead, it felt as though He was directing me to discover His wisdom for myself. I continued to contemplate the question, attempting to find the answer within my own understanding of life. And yet, His silence mimicked the silence within my mind as I reflected upon my finite knowledge of humanity.

In my efforts to find an explanation for my question, I redirected my focus away from myself and The Man, and towards the very people I had created and the lives I had planned out. The reasoning as to why a perfect God would allow an imperfect world to exist potentially dwelled within the confines of my creation. Why would God allow His world to fall into the darkness of sin and transform from paradise into anarchy? Why wouldn't He remove the sin from our nature and return us to the proverbial Garden of Eden? The answers to those ever present questions would soon become apparent.

I started to examine the lives of my creations to better rationalize the often enigmatic logic of God Himself. From my perspective beyond time I could witness the entirety of my creations' existence; their individual births and deaths, each and every moment and decision I had preordained, and the thoughts weren't their own and end of their world. Their lives were entirely perfect, free from pain and sorrow, and despite the mortality of their lifespans, the experiences of loss and heartbreak were absent from their existence as well.

The world beneath me contained a

multitude of people and cultures, formed and structured from the memories I had recalled of my own world. Their ways of life were worlds apart, yet simultaneously formed by the very same creator that shaped the landscape on which they resided. My knowledge laid the foundation of their societies. Cities and industries, relationships and marriages, families and friends; all of which encapsulated the ideals which God had intended for His children before their fall.

Their lives were perfect reflections of God's image, absent of the deadly influence of sin that enveloped the world I had known. Despite the underlying similarities between my creation and the world which I was born into, the absence of pain and loss in the former only further distinguished my work from God's. To be able to see what the world would have been like if not for sin was truly a sight to behold. The perpetual tranquility that was originally intended for God's children had finally become a reality.

There was an inexplicable feeling of grandeur that resided within my heart as I looked upon the seemingly perfect lives of those beneath me. To be able to see individual lives flourish and prosper provided a sense of satisfaction far beyond anything I had known. Emotional turmoil and pain were replaced with peace and happiness. The once inevitable consequential feeling of jealousy that would arise within the hearts of some whenever others achieved something profound or monumental was non-existent. The peace and forgiveness that would have initially been reached though self-sacrifice had become a manifested reality through my own efforts and control.

To create a world so perfect felt like the logical path for a divine creator yet the world I had created appeared to be opposite from what I was born into. In spite of my own feelings of joy as I looked upon my own creation, I remained perplexed as to why God denied Himself and His children such happiness. In my own effort to comprehend God's reasoning, I delved into the complexity of the human nature I had created.

Beyond simply viewing the lives of my creations from my place above and beyond time, I desired to view their existence at their level from the perspective I had always known. With the world's existence on display before me, I decided upon a point in the world's timeline that was most familiar to me. I manifested myself in a developed world; one which I could relate to and understand far better than a moment in the world's beginning or end.

With a single thought I became a part of their world; my world. I could see my creations face-to-face, eye-to-eye. Possessing God's omniscience I could observe my version of humanity from all walks of life and from all corners of the world. In that moment I existed not as a physical embodiment of a person, but as the invisible presence of God that supposedly resided within the world I was born into.

On the surface, the daily lives and conversations of my creations appeared to mirror that of the civilization I was accustomed to. People of all ages and races existed virtually identical to those whom I had known. I was their creator, but I remained among them while retaining my divinity and omnipotence. I looked beyond their physical perspective, peering into the depths of my creations' hearts and minds; both men and women, young and old.

In addition to observing my plans and paths for their lives, I could also gaze into their emotions. The absence of pain and suffering in my world logically resulted in feelings devoid of such negativity. Despite their internal thoughts reflecting the perfection surrounding them, there was a feeling of dissatisfaction within my heart that persisted as I stared into their emotions. This dissatisfied feeling further fed into my desire to discern God's elusive logic.

As I continued my observation, I began

to notice a distinct and linear pattern of thinking shared between all people of the world, virtually identical to the paths I had laid out for their lives. I realized in that moment that their thoughts weren't their own. The same linear paths that I had instantly created for each and every person inevitably resulted in a similarly linear and shallow consciousness. Their lives lacked the depth that I had once believed each individual person possessed. I began to realize their thoughts, their plans and in essence, their will wasn't of their own control, but of mine.

They were simultaneously full of, and void of, life. In theory this shouldn't have been a concern of mine. To be able to accept their apparent lack of free will simply as my own design for their lives would have sufficed, yet despite my desire to accept that notion, I felt as though it was incomplete. Upon my realization of their lack of free will, the feeling of satisfaction that I once felt within my heart slowly dissipated. I halted my attempt to decipher God's reasoning, and began to focus on discerning why I was experiencing a feeling of discontent towards my creations.

I began to expand my horizon, searching not within each person, but instead looking into the world as a whole to ascertain why such a discrepancy existed. In my efforts to find the cause for such discrepancy, I observed the differences that existed between the world of my creation and that of God's. Through my own design for a perfect world, the only experience which could potentially cause the feeling of sorrow and depression was as a result of the death and loss of a loved one. However, even in those instances throughout the world there was only cheerfulness. The mourning that people often felt during tragic moments of loss were replaced with jovial celebrations of life that would contrast such dark periods of grief.

As I gazed upon my creations during their moments of loss, the painful memories of Alexander's short life filled me with emotions that my very creations were unable to experience. In my heart I desired my creations to know the depth of emotions that I was able to feel. However, in order for my creations to understand humanity's full spectrum of emotions I would have to beset them with the same depression that I had fervently prayed for God to remove from my life.

I often desired to experience the same unadulterated joy that I beset upon my creations. To be able to live a life free from the mental distress, pain and loss that has plagued God's creation throughout all of history. Their joy was something I ceaselessly yearned for, yet I began to understand the only reason I had even known that such a joy could exist was a result of the dark and sombre moments of depression I had endured.

The contrast that exists between polar opposite emotions; joy and sorrow, happiness and depression, can only be known by a being with the capacity to experience both sensations. My creations could experience the former, but not the latter, their ignorance was not of their own volition, but of my design. As a consequence of my desires to rid my world of pain and loss, I unknowingly created a humanity that lacked the depth of emotions that God had originally intended for His children.

As I searched my world for pain and heartbreak I only ever found peace and fulfillment. In times that would rationally arise feelings of loss and turmoil, only happiness and joy existed. I desired to create a perfect world, and I succeeded in doing so. My world was devoid of the chaotic storm of emotional distress that I often found myself falling further into. And yet, in the process of forming a flawless reality, one not corrupted by sin, I created a world that was emotionally hollow.

I wanted to be able to feel contentment with my own creation. I wanted to continue to experience the fulfillment I had initially anticipated from forming and shaping a perfect world. Alas, the dissatisfaction that I was inexplicably experiencing continued to persist and grow. Despite how deeply I searched the world before me, a world free from sin and pain, the true answer as to why I was unable to feel satisfied with my creations continued to elude me.

The realization soon dawned on me as I gazed upon my world. Despite my creations living within a perpetual state of bliss, there existed an intrinsic aspect of God's design that was absent from my heart. The foundation of God's relationship with His children was predicated upon His very essence; a foundation that I had cast aside for the sake of manifesting a perfect world. The emotion God endlessly felt for His creation was superficially present in my world, albeit absent from my heart as I looked upon my creation; love.

The love I had designed my creations to feel for themselves and for each other existed. The pure love devoid of jealousy, shared pain and heartache existed within their hearts for their fellow man. And yet, despite my creations only knowing pure, unadulterated love, I was unable to reciprocate such feelings towards them. Their hearts were filled with only a shallow representation of what true love is meant to be. They were unable to know the pain of loss, they couldn't know the wrongdoings caused by love, for in their world 'wrong' did not exist. I designed them to only know of joy and peace, and unfortunately I succeeded.

I was their proverbial father, their creator. The agape love as described in the Bible, the love that transcended boundaries, the love that's shared between a father and his child was all but absent from my relationship with my creations. The knowledge that I was unable to experience the emotional cornerstone of humanity was disheartening. The depth of relationship that can only be formed by a genuine and mutually shared love between a god and his children was absent from my heart, despite my intention to create a world that was entirely without pain and sin. My world was superficially filled with love, but lacked the all encompassing and endless agape love that existed between God and His children.

The cause for my feeling of dissatisfaction towards my creations had become apparent, yet the reason as to why the feeling of genuine love was absent continued to escape me. It was through God's love for His children that He sacrificed His one and only begotten Son to absolve them of their sins, and it's through humanity's desire to know God's love, mercy and purpose for their lives that they would earnestly seek Him. It was a result of each side's willingness to reach for the other that a relationship shared between a creator and the created could exist. And yet, it was a result of my own design and plan that my creations were unable to form such a relationship with me.

I predestined their choices and their paths, I preordained their thoughts and actions. My only intention was to bless them with a perfect life, but only now did I realize that in doing so I had limited the depth of relationship they could experience with me. Despite my efforts to create the world God had initially intended for His children, I had unknowingly prevented my creation from knowing who I was as their proverbial father. I was so fixated on manifesting perfection on their physical world, I never considered allowing my very existence to be known.

I possessed the means to instantly establish a relationship with my creations that mirrored God's relationship with humanity. However, the notion that such a relationship was birthed not through my creation's volition, but through my own omnipotence felt disingenuous. To be predestined to love someone displays only a fragment of what true love and reverence is meant to convey. Even if my creations had the means to love me, but only through my design, the love they would feel would be hollow and superficial. Their love would be devoid of the depth that resides within the wilfully given agape love supposedly shared between God and man.

For even if my creations had the freedom to know me, a consequence of dwelling within a perfect world is the lack of necessity in seeking a divine creator for mercy and direction. Every one of my creations' needs was provided for. The healing many cried out to God for, the wisdom and direction they sought after, and the release of the sin that entangled their souls had already been given prior to my creations' awakening.

My own life was a testament to such a shallow relationship; my only prayers to God were a result of the pain and emotional distress that I could never truly rid myself of. Only in the midst of my depression and emotional struggle did I find myself focusing on my ever fleeting faith in the Lord. The mentality of searching for God in times of trouble wasn't exclusive to myself, however. Testimonies of healing, both Biblical and modern, were often a result of humanity's cry out to God upon reaching a point of mental, physical, emotional or spiritual exhaustion beyond that which they could bear on their own.

In a world devoid of pain and hurt, the desire to seek God's comfort and healing was non-existent. The miraculous and inexplicable healings that occurred throughout history, displaying God's potential for restoration, was absent in my world. The people I created had no need for me to release them of their pain and suffering, as I was the only being within my world who had any knowledge that such a phenomenon could even exist.

Beyond simply lacking the capacity to search after their creator of their own will, I provided no means for my existence to be known. I remained outside of time and beyond the limitations of their understanding. My spirit covered the world, however, my presence remained indiscernible. There was no Bible or holy text within my world, there were no prophets or messiah, there was nothing.

I understood that every prayer to God was not exclusively for healing. God's influence provided direction as much as it provided alleviation of pain. The faith that arose in the notion that a divine plan existed for each and every person was frequently the catalyst which spurred people to further seek the wisdom and guidance of their Heavenly Father.

Only after humanity faithfully submits to God's timing and direction can His plans become actualized. Their submission was a result of trusting that God had laid out a path for their lives greater than they could anticipate and accomplish on their own. Yet, within my world, a similar act of trust was irrelevant. Every path, every decision my creations were to make was predestined to fully realize my greatest intention for their lives. In contrast, faith in God's purpose can often provide justification and comfort for loss and failure. Providing reasoning for such tragedies is entirely unnecessary when the knowledge of such experiences is exclusive to myself.

It was through faith that God's creations could know Him and His plan for their lives. It's through faith that their sins are forgiven and the relationship with God that was severed in the Garden of Eden could be restored. And yet, in my world, faith was inconsequential. The faith that purpose and justification existed in the midst of chaos, and the faith that a divine creator would forgive them of their transgressions was negligible in a world devoid of sin.

As my discontent grew, so too did my desire to create a world of freedom, the same freedom that God had intended and designed for man. I wanted to be able to love my own creation the way God loved His children. I desired my creations to love me as God intended me to love Him. In order for such a genuine and endless agape love to exist, it had to be freely given by those who possessed the sentience to do so.

As I observed my world through the lens of a divine and omnipotent creator, I was becoming enlightened to a depth of God's nature beyond that which I had initially known. Despite my growing wisdom, I still lacked the knowledge to fully comprehend God's divinity. Within the confines of my mind there existed questions that remained unanswered. I returned to my place above and beyond time; the world I had sculpted and the humanity I had formed laid before me.

I stood at the forefront of my creation, their lives and paths still within my command. In order for me to delve further into the depths of God's complexity, I had to create a world of sentience. Through my creations' consciousness could I shape a reality that allowed for the agape love that was denied to my world, and also allowed for freedom, and as a consequence, the potential for pain and suffering. I looked upon the lives of my creations; the individual paths I had laid out, and the perfect plan I had shaped for each person. After a moment of hesitation I wiped away the very same perfect existence I had once desperately yearned for. Each person returned to the emotionless, stagnant state in which they originated. A blank slate existed within each person's heart and mind once more.

The intricate plans I laid out would

eventually be replaced with autonomy and true sentience. Each person possessed the means to shape and forge their lives for themselves. They had the potential to love, discover and inspire, while simultaneously allowing the means for chaos and pain, and the ability to impose their own will upon themselves and others. The perfect world ceased to exist and in its place existed a world full of freedom. A world that, despite the presence of a divine and omnipotent creator, would eventually fall into a greater darkness than I could have ever anticipated.

*

11

Pastor William looked upon the pages in utter confusion. The emotions which he had prayed to God for release of began to resurface as he reached the bottom of the page. Mixed emotions of disbelief and internal contemplation arose; emotions that God had absolved him of, if only as a temporary means for the pastor to be able to receive and understand Jacob's revelation. The pride that existed in the pastor's heart had vanished, yet his belief in God's absolute and unchanging will for humanity remained.

The foundation of the pastor's belief in God's design for man had been criticized beyond anything he had previously experienced. To read that his unwavering faith in God's absolute will for his life was a false doctrine that he had convinced himself of, felt like an affront to his intelligence. Up until that moment the pastor had only ever questioned his current belief to reinforce his own predisposed understanding of God and of the Bible.

His mind and his heart were completely separated and indecisive as a wave of denial began to flood into his mind. He was adamant in his refusal to accept that his previously steadfast knowledge of God's plan and will for his life was incorrect. Yet there was a feeling in his heart that Jacob's story had an authentic merit he couldn't ignore. Regardless as to whether that feeling was through God's influence, or as a faint remnant of the mentality of Arminianism he had once accepted years prior, a seed of doubt was planted within the pastor's heart.

He was lost and uncertain about what he believed to be true. As a pastor it was his responsibility to learn deeper understandings of God's nature and word, and to convey them to his congregation. However, upon reading Jacob's apparent revelation from God Himself, one deeper than anything the pastor had ever experienced, his heart remained hardened and stubborn.

He desired to accept Jacob's revelation, contrary to his own insight about God. Meditating upon his thoughts and feelings the pastor began to question the Bible once more. His questions were rooted in the desire to know if his knowledge of God's word was genuine, or if his long held beliefs were mistaken.

He turned his head towards the right side of his desk. A Bible rested atop a small pile of sermon notes and papers, one the pastor had owned for longer than he could recall. He took hold of the Bible and began to rise from his chair. His back ached once more as he began the arduous process of straightening his spine; an indication he had once again optimism fed than he had realized sitting in front of his desk. With the Bible gripped in his right hand he made his way out of the study and towards the door, leaving behind Jacob's story, open on top of his desk once more.

The sound of classical music could be heard playing from the main floor of the house, as the pastor had come to expect. He began to descend the stairs, which creaked under his weight, mirroring the creaking he felt in his back. As the pastor reached the last step he noticed a singular piece of paper folded upright on the counter in the kitchen. A small plate of breakfast food had been left out from earlier that morning, next to the paper.

He neared the counter and picked up the note left for him:

*I didn't want to disturb you. Make sure to clean up after you eat.
I'll be back later on today, I love you.
-Grace*

Pastor William smiled as he placed the note down and turned his attention towards the plate of food his wife had prepared for him. The plate was filled with typical breakfast foods; cooked eggs and bacon, buttered toast and finely chopped and fried potatoes. The heat that once radiated from the food had all but dissipated. Pastor William turned his attention towards the drawer underneath the note, which housed a variety of cutlery and utensils; the one missing piece Grace had forgot to leave out for her husband.

He grabbed a fork and knife and placed it onto the plate. With his Bible still gripped in his right hand, the pastor took hold of his breakfast and began to walk towards the table near the edge of the kitchen. He placed his food and Bible onto the table, sat down and prayed a short prayer over the food. The pastor opened his Bible; the aged and yellowed pages were stitched in between the worn and cracked bindings. Short hand written notes covered the borders of each page, while underlined and highlighted verses filled each chapter.

Despite the messy appearance of the pages, Pastor William effortlessly navigated his way through the books of the Bible. He attempted to locate specifically highlighted verses that once solidified his own belief and interpretation of God's nature. Excerpts of verses referencing God's children as 'predestined' and 'the elect' began to capture his eyes. The verses that once reinforced the pastor's belief only now resulted in him questioning his own interpretation and knowledge of God's word.

In a race to find Biblical verses that would reinforce his long held belief in God's nature, he came up empty handed, much to his dismay. The passages often cited by those who shared the pastor's outlook appeared insufficient as he reread each verse. As he reviewed each passage, Pastor William was unable to ignore Jacob's claim that, in absence of free will, love is nothing more than an illusion. By the time the pastor cleared his plate, he had reached the conclusion of his Biblical search. He had reread all the verses that had once provided him with such certainty in his understanding of God's nature, yet he remained unsatisfied.

With the plate empty and his Bible closed, Pastor William stood up from his chair feeling disconcerted. He walked away from the table, holding onto his empty plate, while leaving behind his Bible. As he neared the kitchen sink, Grace's note asking the pastor to clean up after his breakfast caught his attention, much to his reluctance. He placed his plate and utensils in the sink as he turned the water tap. A steady stream of hot water soon poured into the sink. Clouds of steam arose, filling the air, much like the thoughts and questions that filled the pastor's mind. After washing, drying and returning his plate and utensils to their proper place, Pastor William returned to the kitchen table to retrieve his Bible before turning around and ascending the staircase to his bedroom.

    He entered the room and placed his Bible onto the nightstand next to his side of the bed. Given his relatively uneventful morning, Pastor William was still clothed in his night wear. The pastor began to pray aloud whilst changing into more casual attire.

    "God, what is the answer that I'm seeking? Why can't I seem to accept everything that was written in Jacob's story? In its essence, it all appears to be in agreement with my understanding of You. Yet at the very end, at the conclusion, Jacob found his creation to be hollow and empty. It just doesn't make any sense to me. It all felt so contrary to my knowledge of You and Your word. Despite

Jacob creating a world devoid of want, need, and sin, he viewed his creation, one of predestination, to be unacceptable. If Jacob couldn't accept his perfect world, how could You accept our own flawed and fallen one? Do You simply possess the means for greater love, or is it maybe due to Jacob's own emotional lacking? God, I want to be able to understand all of this. Jacob put his trust in me to be able to properly utilize his story, yet I'm struggling to even believe it myself. What am I supposed to do...?"

  These prayers remained in the pastor's mind as he walked out of his bedroom and towards his front door. Upon exiting his house, Pastor William began another routine walk around his neighbourhood. The familiar scenery of his neighbourhood was almost entirely ignored as his prayers continued to press against his mind, distracting him from the outside world. Unbeknownst to the pastor, he soon found himself in the seclusion of a local park; a small pocket of nature surrounded by the ambient sounds of both the community and wildlife, a place for him to soak in the intrinsic beauty of God's creation.

  It was during that time that Grace walked through the front door of their house, returning home from her morning errands. As she walked through her house, much to her surprise and appreciation, she noticed that her written request for her husband had actually been fulfilled.

"William?" Grace called out, attempting to discern whether she was alone that afternoon, or if her husband had secluded himself back into his room at the top of the stairs.

There was no response. The house was quiet that afternoon, aside from the classical music playing in the background. Grace ventured up the stairs and peered her head into her husband's study to confirm her suspicion; the sight of the open booklet of papers caught her attention. She entered the empty room to investigate the papers sitting atop the cluttered desk.

She briefly gazed over the wall of text that covered the page, reading but a small fraction of Jacob's story. Upon reaching the bottom of the text Grace instinctively turned the paper, revealing a single white page with four words written in the middle: *'Absolute Freedom And Chaos'* The former half of the title aligning with Grace's belief of God's design for His children, which stood contrary to that which her husband firmly believed.

It was the latter half of the title which transformed her attention into intrigue. She removed the white bookmark from its place at the very beginning of the story before picking up the pile of papers and walking out of the study, towards her bedroom. She had always found the chair in her husband's study to be rather uncomfortable. The old chair had become indented and grooved, contorting to her husband's body and weight over the years. Given Grace's smaller stature, she always felt out of place whenever she attempted to comfortably rest on it; almost as though the chair itself was rejecting her.

She entered into her bedroom and shut the door behind her, a means to better muffle out the classical music she left playing on the main floor of the house. Grace sat on her side of the bed, placed the papers onto her lap and read over the title once more. *'Absolute Freedom And Chaos'*, words that resonated with her, words that would rationally bring forth a surplus of emotions and ideas. Two words that reflected her own belief in God's design, a belief she had formed long ago.

Grace turned to the beginning of the booklet and quickly skimmed through each page. The brief synopsis that Pastor William had given her over dinner allowed her to quickly traverse Jacob's life. Eventually she reached the point at which her husband had previously left off, a blank page with a single word written against a white background: *'Predestination'*. Grace delved into the story Pastor William had already read, yet the two words 'Absolute Freedom' remained at the forefront of her mind.

Reading through Jacob's complications in creating a world absent of free will only further solidified Grace's belief in God's purpose for man. Her belief was not rooted in the knowledge that God had preordained every decision of humanity, but that He could observe every choice they could, and would, make. In her eyes she wasn't a gear in a machine, or an actress in a play, she was a being who possessed the freedom to live a life of her own discretion.

She firmly held onto the notion that if man was made in the image of God, and God Himself had free will, then humanity's own consciousness would reflect that of their Heavenly Father. This was a belief she had formed not out of denial, or a point of nihilism akin to what her husband had experienced. Instead, it was a result of her interpretation of God's word.

Grace's faith was built upon the belief that while God had the potential to bless His children, such blessings were only as a result of their own willingness to seek Him. She didn't pray believing that God had a predetermined plan for her life. Instead, her prayers were for His intervention; for the Lord to show His wisdom amidst an endless array of infinite possibilities.

Her belief was predicated not in the understanding that sin and pain were simply an aspect of 'God's will' for humanity, but instead out of acceptance that God had given humanity the freedom to choose Himself or the world; salvation or sin. She believed that humanity was in control of their own destiny, and that God would only direct and influence those who sought after Him.

The fundamental belief Grace held in regard to her interpretation of God's will was, in essence, the main divide that existed within her marriage, but was also the very foundation of the couple's relationship. Opposite interpretations and understandings of God's word had the potential to cause an unbridgeable gap between the two, especially given her husband's position in their church and his steadfast belief. However, The philosophical and theological debates that frequently occurred within the walls of their house wasn't a cause for division. Instead, their mutual faith in God and Christ, and the deep love for one another allowed their marriage to thrive despite their differing views.

Contrary to her husband, Grace viewed the chaos and disorder throughout the world, not as a result of God's discretion, but instead as a consequence of humanity's freedom in God's world. In her mind, believing that the pain and suffering within the world was nothing more than God's will seemed contrary to the notion that God loved and cared for mankind. She was unable to accept that an all loving and all powerful God would intentionally design His creation to defile His nature.

Grace felt that those who prayed for God's intervention in their lives, while simultaneously believing that His will was predetermined, were contradicting themselves. She would frequently pray alongside her husband, often with shared intention, but the foundation of their prayers was mutually exclusive. Throughout the early years of their marriage, despite their differing views, they routinely prayed with a singular intention; a desire that resided within both of their hearts, yet remained beyond their reach: a family.

Her greatest desire, and her greatest ambition in her life was a catalyst for her deepest prayers, but also her greatest pain. She continually sought for God's intervention in her life, yet He remained absent. For much of her life Grace yearned and prayed for the blessing of motherhood. To be able to raise and nurture a family and to bear the responsibility of parenting. It was her greatest ambition, but for reasons beyond her or her husband's control, she was denied the means to walk down that path in life. In her eyes, accepting such a circumstance as "God's will" appeared to simply be an easy way out; a means for someone to cast away their frustrations whilst refusing to question such an outcome.

For God to intentionally place an endless desire into someone's heart while simultaneously denying them the means to fulfill said desire felt nothing short of cruel in her eyes. Both Grace and Pastor William had sought God in their initial efforts to bear children, continually praying and reading God's word in hopes of receiving such a blessing. The accounts of Biblical women who themselves experienced the pain of barrenness only to receive God's blessing reinforced Grace's faith. Yet in the midst of their efforts a darkness began to develop. A darkness which would quickly strip Grace of her dreams and leave her physically and emotionally barren.

The disappointment that existed within the heart of Pastor William paled in comparison to the pain that Grace had felt. Pastor William's comfort was rooted in the belief that God had preordained such an outcome, yet in Grace's eyes this was simply God denying her the blessing she had fervently prayed for. Either possibility led to an equally harsh reality; continually praying for God's blessing only to be left empty handed and distraught.

Grace refused to accept that God would have placed such a desire in her heart knowing full well such an outcome would never come to fruition. She believed her initial aspiration for motherhood was her own, birthed from her own free will. It was through her own free will that she sought after God's influence, and yet though God's own freedom that her prayer for His intervention was for naught.

Her faith in God persisted despite the outcome. However the aftermath only further reinforced her belief that her desires and God's decision was a result of their free will. The freedom to wilfully give and receive blessings, while allowing the potential for pain and loss despite an all-loving God, was only possible within a world of self-awareness, sentience, and free will. The unmistakable knowledge that the world was indiscriminate in its turmoil and that God's influence only seemed to occur infrequently further fed into Grace's belief.

It was her faith in free will that granted Grace an answer to the endless questions of theodicy and the ever present problem of evil. It was a result of humanity's actions and sinful nature that brought about their destruction, and the ceaseless chaos in the world was a consequence of humanity's unchecked freedom. She viewed the disarray that encompassed the world simply as a reflection of the sin that resided within each person's soul. As Grace saw it, the natural disasters, sickness and havoc in the world were not brought upon by a passive, unloving God, but by a God who's desire for mankind's free will surpassed His desire to dictate their lives.

    While Grace's belief was formed as a result of her interpretation of God's word, its foundation was rooted from a more defining, tragic moment of her life. It was a moment of both loss and healing, that despite occurring forty years ago still remained fresh in Grace's mind.

    Grace and her husband had waited in the doctor's office, anxiety and uncertainty growing within their hearts with each passing second. The atmosphere was heavy and the silence seemed to be all encompassing, save for the subtle ticking of a clock affixed to the wall. Each minute felt like an hour. An endless stream of thoughts and worries paraded through the young couple's minds. The accumulating dread slowly eroded away any remaining optimism they once had.

    Grace's dreams and ambitions hindered on the coming moments. The days prior were filled with fearful anticipation and concern, feelings which crescendoed as their appointment drew closer. They waited in silence, uncertain about how much time had passed since they had first sat down in the empty room.   Fear immediately gripped Grace's heart as their doctor entered her office.

"I'm sorry to keep you waiting." the doctor apologized. The subtle lilt in her voice carried a seriousness that further confirmed Grace's fear and anxiety.

The doctor sat down in front of the couple, closed her eyes before uttering two words that caused Grace's stomach to drop and her heart to sink deep into her chest; 'I'm sorry.'

In a single moment her fears had become a reality. The sound of the doctor's voice began to fade as a storm of distress and hopelessness flooded into her mind. Her greatest ambition and the dreams which she had held for as long as she could remember were suddenly stripped away. She sat expressionless; emotionless. The doctor continued to speak, but the words were unable to reach Grace's ears. The confirmation that the young couple would be denied the means to bear children erased any semblance of optimism they once had for a family.

The doctor continued to speak, her words carrying a weight greater than anything the couple thought they could bear. A singular word stood out from the doctor's diagnosis: cancer. The shock of her diagnosis cut through Grace's grief, and transformed her anxiety into fear. Time stood still as her world shattered around her. Grace remained consumed with grief and sorrow until the doctor had finished her prognosis.

"Again, I'm so sorry." The doctor lamented.

"Thank you for your time," Pastor William muttered, holding back tears.

The couple stood up from their seats after bidding the doctor a sombre goodbye. The pastor gripped his wife's hand tightly in a feeble attempt to comfort her as they exited the doctor's office. The car ride back to their house was entirely silent. The encroaching darkness of night mirrored the emotional desolation that Grace was internally experiencing. Any semblance of optimism the couple once had was extinguished. Only silence remained as they pulled into their driveway. Pastor William cut the engine and turned to his wife, her expression remained unchanged since their appointment.
She stepped out from the car and walked towards their house, leaving her husband sitting alone. After unlocking the door, she entered the house. The emptiness and silence in their home only served as a reminder to Grace of what she had lost.

Grace began to walk up the stairs towards her bedroom, the weight of her circumstances seemed to grow with each step. She closed the door behind her, the sound of it shutting reverberated through the house. There was an unspoken understanding between the couple that their bedroom room would remain closed until Grace herself opened it up again.

The self isolation Grace placed herself in following her return home was broken only by her routine trips to the hospital for treatment. The times she spent alone in her home focused her attention in one of two directions. The pain in her heart seemed to be all consuming, yet she remained steadfast and focused on her faith in God. During that time, at the lowest moments of Grace's life she called out to God for healing, both to be released of the pain in her heart and of the disease ravaging her body.

The bleak atmosphere in the house lingered in the coming days. According to their doctor the chances for Grace's survival were quite high, mitigating her husband's concern, if only slightly. However, Grace's fear for her life persisted, despite the reassurance of her doctor. She knew that while her physical health could be restored, the pain gripping her heart would persist for the remainder of her life.

In the coming days and weeks, Grace's time was split between the isolation of her home and the hospital for treatments. During her treatments, her mind was torn between her physical circumstances and her relationship in God. With each consecutive appointment, the doctors and nurses' optimism towards Grace's health and recovery dwindled.

They attempted to remain positive in an effort to reassure Grace of the situation, but she saw through their facade. Her depleting optimism fed into the fear festering within her heart, but also drew Grace closer to God. As her fear began to grow, so too did her faith; the last remaining beacon of hope she held onto in the midst of her dire circumstances.

Grace's faith persisted amid her illness. She unequivocally trusted that God possessed the capability to release her from the grip of this terminal disease, despite the doubt that dwelled within the hearts of the medical staff. She placed her faith in God, and either through her own submission, or through God's desire to answer her cries, God began to intervene.

Midway through her treatment procedure she was called into the doctor's office. Looking upon Grace's test results, the doctor sat in bewilderment at what she read. In front of her sat a woman who was once plagued with a terminal disease, yet was seemingly alleviated from every trace of the illness.

Grace's sudden healing was a medical anomaly; one that arose feelings of disbelief within Grace and her doctor, yet one neither of them could deny. The miraculous answer to her prayers was a testament of God's intervention, yet despite being cleansed of her cancer, the scars in her body remained. She was still denied her greatest dream, her life's ambition, despite experiencing something that could only be described as a miracle. Her story was an account of divine intervention, one that countless people pray for, yet few truly experience.

She continued to cry out to God for a full restoration of her body. However, despite praying with the same intensity that brought forth God's initial intervention, her calls to God remained unanswered. 'Time heals all wounds' was an adage that Grace desperately wanted to accept; for time to run its course and to be released from the pain dwelling within her heart. She waited with faithful anticipation that God would once again divinely restore to Grace that which was corrupted and removed.

Yet as the days passed, the anticipation and expectation Grace firmly held onto began to lose momentum. In its wake, the reality of her new circumstances overtook her focus, allowing a myriad of emotions to manifest themselves within her heart. The optimism and eager anticipation Grace had towards the future transitioned into a bleak and barren outlook of the coming days. Her prayers for healing and restoration soon became prayers for God's comfort in her new reality. Yet despite experiencing circumstances that would often silence one's faith, Grace's faith persisted. She understood that despite her inability to bear children, she was miraculously healed from a disease that had claimed the lives of countless people.

Unlike her husband, Grace didn't accept that she was healed as a result of God's divine plan. Instead, she believed that her healing was a result of her willingness to reach out to her Heavenly Father. Her restoration set the foundation for her belief, not just in her own free will in God's wilful intervention.

In Grace's eyes the miraculous healings which occurred throughout history were not solely a result of man's faith in God, but through God's own willingness to heal those who cried out to Him. For if humanity had the freedom to genuinely and earnestly cry out to God in times of pain and distress, then God possessed the freedom to answer or deny their prayers.

Grace often wrestled with her own understanding as to why an all-loving God would often deny the prayers of humanity. The logic of God's rationale alluded her, yet as she reached the conclusion of Jacob's account of predestination, she gained deeper insight into God's nature than she previously understood. She turned the page over, revealing the four words that remained the focus of her attention; *'Absolute Freedom And Chaos'*. After flipping over the title, Grace turned her eyes to the top of the page before beginning the next chapter of Jacob's account.

12

*

-Absolute Freedom And Chaos-

I looked upon my creation. The limitless potential of each person laid before me, the entirety of their lives were within my command. I would soon bless my creations with the means to manifest their own desires and ambitions; a blessing of freedom and sentience that was once absent from their lives.

Seated above and beyond time, I could again observe the entirety of existence; from its initial moment of creation to its conclusion. As I gazed into the heart and soul of each person, I was able to see a void; an empty canvas of infinite possibilities. My once intricate and complex orchestration of humanity was gone, yet in its place existed the potential for my creations to know a life beyond anything they had experienced. The path for their lives was to be decided, not by my own omnipotence, but by the absolute freedom of each individual person.

I knew what I wanted to accomplish. I understood how to instill free will within the life of each person. Yet, despite possessing the means to bless my creation with sentience, I felt a sense of hesitation welling within my heart. My hesitancy was brought upon by my previous experience in giving life to my creations. I knew that despite my efforts to actualize perfection, I only created a world devoid of genuine love.

My reluctance grew as my thoughts lingered. My past failure in manifesting the world I had longed for weighed upon my heart. I wanted to create and bless my creation with freedom, but instead I was struggling to act upon the freedom I personally possessed. Either due to His understanding of my circumstance, or simply a result of His omnipotence, The Man spoke,

"Why do you hesitate?" He asked.

"I don't know," I replied, still searching for an answer. "I know that no matter what happens I still control their world, but for some reason I almost feel too

scared to actually do anything."

"What is it that you fear?"

"I'm not sure. I want to love my world, and to feel the love that God has for His children, but for some reason I'm struggling to let my creations love me."

"Your hesitation is rooted in your concern for their well being." He reassured, *"You had initially blessed your creations with perfect lives. However, now that they possessed the means to live a life of pain and hardship you're reluctant in going forth with your decision."*

"I think so." I admitted.

"Just as darkness can only truly be known in a world in which light is present, genuine love can only exist within a world that understands pain and loss."

"I understand, I just don't want to see people go through the same pain that I prayed to be healed of." My apprehension began to seep into my tone.

"You already feel some semblance of love towards your creation, now is the time to allow them to feel that same love for you."

"Alright, I'll give it a try."

The hesitation I felt remained present, still lingering in my heart. And yet, I knew that the wisdom and understanding I sought could only be discovered by granting my creations free will. Before me lay the foundation of creation; a blank slate of limitless possibilities. Each person possessed the means to alter and direct their lives by their own design.

As a result of their freedom, my creations possessed the potential to instill their own will onto themselves and others. They had the capability to become a blessing or a curse to those around them; a choice for them to make by their own volition. Beyond free will, I also instilled a sense of morality akin to the morality that I myself possessed. My creation's morality was based upon my own sense of judgment and righteousness, one rooted in the Biblical values that lay as the foundation in my own life.

Shortly after instilling the potential for free will and morality within my creation I returned my focus to the beginning of time; the beginning of my creation's existence. With a single thought I brought every person, every being, to life. Their decisions and choices would be entirely of their own volition. In my divinity I understood each and every person's aspirations and desires; everyone's fears and concerns. As I further examined the extent of what I had endowed into my creations, I began to see the rippling effects of their sentience and freedom through the passing of time.

The actions and consequences of my

creations were of their own accord. Millions of people shaped the lives of themselves and others with every decision. Resting above time, I could see a darkness looming in the distance. Within the darkness was a world overrun with disparity and destruction, pain and death; the very antithesis of my initial creation.

Through my omniscience, I could hear and witness the anguish that my creations were enduring; the sorrow and depression they felt and the pain they suffered. Their cries for release of their circumstances resonated into the fibres of my being. I desired to create a world that could wilfully experience my love; a world that could love me as man loved God. Yet, despite my greatest intentions, the world before me remained rife with grief and pain.

The question of how a simple blessing of freedom resulted in unending chaos lingered in my mind. I attempted to mirror the autonomy that God had bestowed on man, yet my creation's unchecked freedom resulted in a world drowning in destruction. Despite believing that I had gained God's wisdom as a result of my initial creation, I was still left bereft of an answer as to why my world had fallen into darkness. I was lost, searching for an answer. Being entirely aware of the uncertainty and concern welling within my heart, The Man began to speak to me once again.

"What is pressing on your mind?" He asked

"What's happening? Why is everything falling apart?" I questioned, my voice gripped with concern and worry.

"The all consuming darkness that you see is a visual manifestation of sin itself. The cries you hear is your creations succumbing and suffering from the sin surrounding them. As time progresses and sin becomes more rampant so too does the darkness become more suffocating, and their cries become more desperate. Only when the darkness fully consumes their lives will their cries fall silent."

"What am I supposed to do?" I asked, witnessing my creations' unending suffering, "Can't I just forgive my creations and remove their sins?"

"Your forgiveness erases humanity's sin from your eyes, but it does not absolve man of the transgressions he committed against another."

"Am I just supposed to let them suffer?"

"Their suffering will last as long as you allow, but the answer you seek is not embedded in their lack of suffering."

"And where am I supposed to find this

answer?"

"Observe their world before you." The Man directed, "The fall of humanity is rooted in their nature."

I peered into the hearts and minds of my creations.

"The answer you're seeking is one that you're to discover on your own." The Man continued, "My only intention is to provide you with the means to discover what you're searching for."

"I don't really understand. Why can't You just tell me what I'm looking for?"

"Yours is a question regarding the nature of humanity and of freedom. A simple explanation wouldn't suffice, not compared to the wisdom that can be gained through witnessing and experiencing the divinity of God firsthand."

I continued to look at the world before me. The darkness encompassing it became far more imposing with each passing moment.

"So I'm supposed to discover the reason why the world has fallen into sin myself?"

"Because the revelation and understanding you seek is far greater than that which can be deciphered through conversation, you must witness the cause for sin firsthand. Only then will you be able to truly know both the workings of God and the

realities of humanity."

"Is that the purpose for this revelation? Just so I can see why people sin?"

"The answer to your questions will be given in time. Only after you learn of the world and human nature will you understand both the reasoning and the purpose for why you are to receive such a revelation."

"Is there anything that You can do to at least point me in the right direction?"

"Look towards the beginnings of life. That is where you shall find the origin of their sin."

My eyes became fixated on the beginning of time, the very moment before I had awoken my creations.

"So the answer I'm looking for is there?"

"Yes. By witnessing humanity's sin you shall gain the understanding you seek."

"Alright, if You say so." I said, continuing to look upon my world.

I turned my attention to the full timeline of my creation, seeking the answer The Man eluded to. In the beginning existed a world teeming with endless possibilities. While my initial creation dwelled within a reality that was devoid of pain and sorrow, my new world was brimming with the full spectrum of human emotion. My world mirrored that of the world which God had created, and my inhabitants were a reflection of the Lord's children. The potential for pain existed within both the world I was born into and the world I had created. However, the melancholy and sorrow that existed within the former paled in comparison to the darkness that would befallen my world.

Through my omniscience I could witness every potential choice, every possible decision and consequence for my creations. Their lives were no longer linear, but multidimensional. Their choices were of their own free will, but despite viewing the near infinite possibilities of humanity's timeline, it seemed that every timeline, save for one mirroring the world I had previously manifested, would eventually experience a creeping darkness that grew over time. Each one of the near infinite timelines all initially housed the potential to reach the same perfect world I had first created. However, despite their freedom to achieve perfection, almost every timeline fell short.

I was unable to understand how such an initially peaceful world could sink into such depravity. Once again, I desired to see the world from humanity's perspective; to be able to witness firsthand how a world formed and shaped by a divine being could descend into a broken state of existence. I returned to the surface of the world once more, wanting to view my fallen world from the perspective of its inhabitants.

The entirety of the world's population surrounded me. Just as my presence surrounded the surface of the planet, so too did my vision. I could witness every corner of the world simultaneously. The multitude of people, societies and cultures that existed around the world was nearly identical to the world I had known. However, through my omniscience I could see a depth of reality far beyond anything I could have anticipated.

The linear world and timeline that I had once experienced had been replaced with a sight beyond comprehension. Layers upon layers of alternate timelines existed, each one born out of the endless possibilities of humanity's sentience. The billions of connected and interconnected lives that I had witnessed previously was but an infinitesimal fraction of the limitless complexity that laid before my eyes. The endless series of possibilities was birthed not from my omnipotence, but of the innumerable choices that humanity had made since the very beginning of their history. Small insignificant choices had the potential to ripple into outcomes far greater than they could have ever anticipated; for better or for worse.

As the lives of my creations began to take form, their societies, cultures and ways of life appeared virtually identical to that which I had first expected. The initial stages of my creation's existence matched the world which I had always known; a world full of both pain and joy, heartbreak and celebration. The essence of life that my initial creations were denied of, was instilled in the world before me. Despite my intentions, my creation's fall into depravity became more apparent with the passing of each generation.

The darkness of sin was faint in the beginning of time. However, as time progressed the darkness and anarchy steadily grew. The transition from joy and happiness to pain and sorrow began to escalate, shaking the foundation of my creation. Eventually a blanket of chaos would be cast upon them that would eventually bring forth their own self-destruction.

The fear and concern I felt became a reality as I looked upon the timeline of my creation. Within my effort to shape a world with the potential to experience the full extent of human emotion, I unwittingly brought about their demise. The world which I was born into and the world I had created were one and the same, virtually identical in their cultures and societies. And yet, despite their near identical foundations, the beings in my world bestowed upon themselves a torment beyond anything I could have envisioned.

In addition to corrupting humanity, the darkness of sin spread into the depths of the planet itself. While the inhabitants dwelling atop the surface of the world were of my creation, the world itself was birthed from The Man's omnipotence. It was His perfect creation which was slowly suffocating from the deathly grip of sin. With each generation of man, the influence of sin became more powerful. As the intensity of sin grew, so too did the frequency of the natural disasters and sicknesses that plague humanity. The Biblical descriptions of a devastating flood mirrored the catastrophic disasters that bombarded my creations. It appeared as though the world itself was attempting to erase the cancerous plague residing atop its surface.

The ferocity of the storms and the lethality of the sicknesses became more rampant as the darkness of sin grew. Just as I commanded the wind and the waves, so too did my creations' freedom affect the world around them. They were the arbiters of their own destruction, while remaining ignorant of the consequences of their actions.

The curse of sin echoed throughout the world, its deadly claws sinking further into The Man's creation, corrupting every corner of the planet. A single sin would ripple outward, endlessly expanding and gaining momentum until it became uncontrollable. The origin of sin in my world was not a singular act of defiance as depicted in the Bible. Instead, it was a result of a continual gradation of actions that were in direct disobedience to the natural consciousness and morality I had bestowed within my creations. As my creations were made in my image, so too did their morality reflect my own view of righteousness.

Their sin was a violation of the moral law I had bestowed within their hearts; an act of rebellion committed against themselves and others. It was a result of their defiance that brought upon the darkness of sin, and eventually their own demise. The consequences of their actions had the potential to falter societies and to alter the natural landscape of the world. Even small acts of rebellion predicated by good intentions housed the potential to further spread the darkness of sin.

While my creation's vision was limited, I could witness events far beyond their perception. Beyond simply assuming the results of their actions, I could witness the consequences of their decisions. For every option that lay before my creations and every choice they could make, I could witness every possible outcome simultaneously. All actions brought forth consequences, and all acts had the potential to ripple into the future. The answers to theodicy I sought were within my grasp, formed by my growing understanding of human nature and witnessing the results of their existence and of their free will.

The evil and sin that existed within my world was frequently the result of my creations' inability to comprehend their actions. Though my creation's conscience provided them an innate sense to distinguish right from wrong, they lacked the wisdom to understand why actions were of the former or latter. As a result of my creation's limited understanding of morality, their interpretation and justifications for their actions allowed sin to corrupt their world. They could inherently see the act of murder and theft to be a violation of the morality they were endowed with. However, by finding rationale for their actions, they began to blur the lines between righteousness and evil, until my morality was nothing more than an afterthought.

While my creations' freedom had the potential to cause either good or evil, it also allowed the means to seek a higher power in their times of strife and anguish. I could hear the prayers of those around me, witness those who earnestly cried out to me. Despite their inability to even know of my existence, as the darkness of sin became greater, so too did their cries to a higher power become more earnest.

Beyond hearing their prayers, I could witness the potential repercussions the answers they desired would bring forth. I understood that their prayers held the potential to create good will and shine light in the darkness of their would. Yet, my understanding of the future and the results of such answers denied me the willingness to respond to their cries.

I understood that though my creation's cries were genuine, the immediate answers to their prayers had the means to deny them a greater blessing, or inadvertently cause the darkness of sin to grow. At that moment I began to fully realize why God seemed to ignore the prayers of man. God had the means to see into the infinite possibilities of humanity, and to fully comprehend the repercussions of their actions. In my divinity I held the foundation to the answer of theodicy, yet I was alone in this understanding. In addition to their prayers for healing and direction, as time progressed and the darkness of sin grew, their prayers for understanding of why such sin and pain existed became more frequent.

Beyond witnessing the consequences of my creations' actions, I could also see the effect that my own influence would have within their world. Direct contact with my very essence would be beyond their comprehension. Physically witnessing and experiencing my full divinity would result in a world so enamoured by my presence that it would have no choice but to acknowledge my sanctity and adhere to my morality. Knowing that an omnipotent being was among them would have consequently resulted in a wilful submission of their freedom, ultimately returning them back to their initial state of lifeless obedience.

As I listened to my creations cry out amidst the darkness, I began to realize they possessed the cornerstone of religion; faith. Faith, not in a God they had come to know, but faith in a higher power. My creations sought a cause and a purpose for their existence and their suffering. Yet despite their prayers, I was beyond their understanding and comprehension. They had no knowledge of my existence, yet they cried for me. They cried into the endless void of their reality in an effort to find reasoning for the sin and corruption in their world. They sought after a God they didn't know and for a purpose and plan that didn't exist. Despite it all, they had faith in me.

I had arrived at a crossroads; two separate paths laid before me, each one with its own consequences and repercussions. I could answer my creations' cries, reveal myself and bring forth the peace, tranquility and perfection that I had initially created. In doing so I could bless my creations with a world where the darkness of sin had been extinguished and their pain was erased. Yet in doing so I would remove my creation's ability to utilize the free will I had bestowed upon them.

Alternatively, by remaining beyond their knowledge, they would continue to spiral down the endless void of sin and death. Their actions would allow the darkness covering their world to grow and ultimately lead to their own self-destruction. I was uncertain of what I desired to become of my creations. The ever present darkness loomed in the distance, while the knowledge I had gained and the regret I felt from the creation of my last world, one devoid of free will, continued to weigh upon my mind.

Against my better judgment I decided to follow the latter of the two paths. My influence would remain as nothing more than a simple and rare occurrence; only accessible to those who truly cried out to me and would only be brought about by my willingness to heed their cries. My intervention would only be used as a means to positively influence the lives of my creations, even if not initially obvious from their limited perspective.

I remained as an invisible and intangible force, existing beyond my creations' physical senses. Having decided my course of action I returned my focus to the physical world before me. What I witnessed provided me with the insight I sought after and the understanding as to why the darkness of sin became more suffocating as time passed. The myriad of decisions my creations made throughout their existence dictated the societies and cultures they lived within. They could choose what they believed to be righteous and just, despite the morality I had bestowed within their hearts.

The moral compass I had instilled in my creations initially laid the foundation of their societies and shaped their ways of life, but as time progressed, their cultural values would overtake their sense of righteousness. As the generations would come and go, their moral instincts would slowly become compromised. The further societies would distance themselves from my morality, the more influence sin had over their world. Justification would soon overtake their willingness to judge righteous and evil behaviour for what it truly is. Their sense of justice and wickedness became twisted and perverted as sin slowly began to corrupt their very nature, silencing their consciousness and misshaping their morality.

While many would be willing to hold firmly to their morality, without a clear foundation as to the origin of their innate sense of justice, the once pure and innocent nature of humanity became lost. I remained in the midst of a transforming landscape, devolving into a world unrecognizable from its initial creation. Within their fallen world righteous living was viewed as foolish, while perverse lifestyles of wickedness and debauchery were normalized. In spite of their actions I could sense an unspoken storm of conflicting emotions within the hearts and minds of my creations.

In my creation's freedom they had the means to indulge in actions they understood to be wrong. They knowingly and wilfully brought about their own self destruction by embracing lives that would only further bring them down into the depths of sin. As their generations progressed they bore witness to the gradual and continual fall of their civilizations. Despite defiling their morality while witnessing the destruction of their world, they continually declared their innocence.

My creations cried out to me for release from their pain and sorrow, while their actions fed into the cloud of darkness consuming their lives. They prayed for healing, but refused to cut themselves off of the very source of their pain. While I desired to answer their prayers I remained silent amidst their cries.

I gazed into my world beyond what my creations could see and I bore witness to the multitude of possibilities derived from my creations' freedom. The increasing darkness covering their world correlated with the depression and nihilism forming within their souls. The corruption of sin I could observe at the conclusion of humanity's timeline reflected the dark emotions harbouring within the hearts and minds of each and every one of my creations.

Their mental and emotional state declined as time progressed, bringing forth a crippling depression within their hearts that slowly seeped into the world around them. As I witnessed their pain and sorrow, I began to experience a strong emotion welling within my heart; empathy. Their suffering and depression was virtually identical to the emotional storm I had previously endured. I desired to help them, I desired to alleviate them of their pain and suffering, but in my omniscience I understood that my intervention would cause unwanted ramifications.

The empathy I felt towards my creation tore my heart asunder. I wanted to absolve them of the pain they were enduring, yet I desired my creations to retain their freedom. I wished to prevent my creations from falling down the dark chasm of sin and death, yet I refused to dictate their lives and deny them their sentience.

I remained at an impasse. I could either allow my creations to live in a world absent of consciousness, or grant them the means to indulge in the limitless freedom that could bring about their own destruction. In those moments I began to slowly draw closer to the final conclusion; the revelation that was intended for me since the moment I had first awoken in the meadow.

I desired to provide my creations with a reality in which they could be free from sin and darkness, while retaining their freedom and sentience. I looked upon my creations, peering into the slate of infinite possibilities within their heart. I had intended to correct the mistakes I made when I first acted as God over their world. Their lives remained within my command, and in a single instance the canvas that once displayed the limitless possibilities of each person's life was empty once again.

*

13

The light of the late afternoon sun shone through the bedroom window. Grace took her eyes off of the story before placing it on her lap and returning her attention back towards the world. Sitting in silence, Grace reflected upon Jacob's writing. His description of free will mirrored Grace's belief of God's design for humanity. Everything she had read fit perfectly into her understanding of the world and of God, yet the unintended consequences Jacob had described roused doubts within her heart; a feeling her husband had also been wrestling with.

Within her mind, the beginnings of

self-doubt began to take shape. What she initially believed to be a confirmation of her steadfast belief, instead resulted in questioning her understanding of God's design. While Grace struggled to agree with her husband's belief in predestination, Jacob's criticism of free will began to cast doubts on her own understanding. Despite the continual debates Grace had had with her husband regarding God's design for humanity, for the first time in recent years she felt uncertain about what she believed.

  Recalling the previous night, Grace began to understand why her husband had appeared so distant during the evening. Having read Jacob's criticism of both predestination and free will, she sympathized with the despondency her husband was enduring. Just as the pastor's beliefs were scrutinized, so too were Grace's. She had always believed that the blessing of absolute free will was God's ultimate gift to man; a means to live a life without requiring God's continual intervention. She accepted that sin, and the defilement of God's law was a consequence of humanity's freedom and sentience. However, to be told that in a world of absolute free will, sin would run rampant and eventually bring forth humanity's destruction, stood in the face of everything she thought she had understood.

While Grace was aware that she may not fully understand the depth of God's design for humanity, Jacob's story only caused her to further question her belief. For the first time, the criticism she received was not from someone who openly disagreed with her understanding of humanity's design. Instead, the origin of the criticism was from someone who desired Grace's belief of absolute, unchecked freedom to be true.

Grace stood up, her neck was faintly stiff from her time reading Jacob's story. She stretched out her arms in front of her as she began to walk away from her bed, the papers firmly held in her left hand. The hinges began to creak as she steadily opened the door before stepping out from her bedroom. Peering into her husband's study she could see him hunched over his desk, reading from the open Bible before him, entirely unaware his wife was looking in.

"William?" Grace asked.

Pastor William remained unfazed, completely fixated on his Bible.

"William!" Grace called out.

Breaking the pastor's focus, he turned to his wife standing in the door frame; the familiar papers gripped in her hand.

"I saw you reading that after I returned home." He remarked while eyeing the papers, "You looked so peaceful, I didn't want to disturb you."

"That's very kind of you. I may return the favour one day." she jested.

"What do you think of it so far?" Pastor William asked through his smile.

"It's thought provoking to say the least, but I can see why you're so focused on it. I just hope you don't find it more interesting than your dear sweet wife."

"You don't have to worry about that. It hopefully shouldn't be too much longer before I've finished it."

"I just hope I won't be waiting on you for too long." Grace replied, handing the papers over to her husband. "It'll be a little while before dinner's ready, maybe you can use that time to catch up." she teased, pointing towards her bookmark placed several pages ahead of her husband's.

Pastor William smiled, graciously accepting his wife's challenge while placing the papers next to his Bible. Grace closed the door behind her as she walked out of the room before descending the staircase. Upon reaching the main floor of their house, she made her way towards the kitchen and began to prepare an evening dinner for herself and her husband. The leftover roast sat in the refrigerator; a prime ingredient for a stew Grace had been craving.

As Grace's cooking progressed,

thoughts and questions pertaining to Jacob's story arose within her mind. Her internal dialogue began to rationalize the apparent revelation Jacob had documented. In her mind it all felt so outlandish, so improbable, yet in contrast to the miraculous healing she had been blessed with, Jacob's revelation and experience seemed all the more believable.

Her mind began to wander down a series of rabbit holes, every thought leading down a path of various philosophical and religious questions and discussions. She reflected upon the questions that would frequently arise at one time or another during the debates Grace shared with her husband. The arguments that initially confirmed her belief felt hollow and ineffective as she pondered Jacob's story.

Time seemed to pass quickly as the evening drew closer. Standing at the edge of the kitchen table Grace placed the two bowls of stew onto it's wooden surface. At that very moment within his study, Pastor William rested his bookmark next to his wife's. Situated directly underneath the black and white bookmarks was the title of the next chapter of Jacob's account: *'My Will'*. The pastor pushed himself away from his desk, while stretching out his stiffened arms. Standing upright, he returned his chair to its place underneath the desk, before a sudden knock on the door caught his attention.

"Mr. Peterson, your dinner is ready." Grace jokingly called to her husband, her voice slightly muffled by the closed door between them.

"I'll be right there," he responded, his hand still resting atop the back of the chair.

Pastor William descended the staircase and walked into the kitchen, where his wife was patiently waiting for him. Looking up towards her husband Grace began to speak,

"I'm glad you decided to join me. I'm starting to think you're more interested in that story than me." she jested.

"You don't have to worry about that, my dear." he responded.

Pastor William took his seat, the stiffness still lingering in his joints. After taking a moment to adjust, he briefly prayed over their meal before delving into a discussion of the very subject that remained at the forefront of the couple's minds.

"So, what did you think of Jacob's apparent revelation so far?" Pastor William asked.

"I'm confused to say the least. I've been thinking about what we were talking about last night and I'm starting to understand why you seemed so distracted after dinner. I'm starting to feel that way myself. It's interesting, it feels like Jacob touched on a lot of what I believe, while turning everything on its head."

"That's certainly one way to put it," the pastor conceded. "I'm still wrestling with it all. If it's nothing more than a dream, then I can accept it as just another belief. However, if what Jacob wrote is true, then it makes me question everything that I already believe. I know you and I have had these conversations many times before, but for the first time in a while I'm struggling to rationalize my beliefs."

"I think it's because it feels honest, almost transparent." Grace said, reaching for her glass as water, "It's not as though Jacob is claiming that he's correct, or that his revelation is the God given truth. In fact, I appreciate that he openly acknowledged his own faults and doubts through it all. It doesn't seem like he's trying to convince anyone of anything, it doesn't even feel like he's speaking on his own behalf. Instead, it feels like he's wrestling with the same issues you and I have been talking about for a while now."

"Do you think there's any merit to Jacob's story?" Pastor William asked, a spoonful of stew hovering in front of his mouth.

"I think it's possible, although I'm still trying to figure out what I actually believe. I know you and I don't always see eye to eye in this, but the more I think about what Jacob's claims, the more I'm starting to accept that

God may actually have some influence in our lives. But, the whole idea that God has only one plan for our lives feels too limiting to me."

Pastor William placed his spoon onto the table.

"I get it, I really do. I understand your beliefs, but I can't simply let go of the idea that God has control over our lives. The healing He blessed you with, the life He's given us, I can't imagine any of this happening without His direct control. And yet..."

"And yet," Grace interrupted, "Jacob's revelation flies in the face of everything you believe. You desperately want to be right, yet when you're told that you might be wrong by the very same God we both believe in, you find yourself struggling to accept it."

"It's not as though I'm against changing my mind," the pastor defended himself, "It's just that everything about it feels so improbable."

Grace took a sip from her glass of water before responding to her husband.

"You say that, yet you acknowledge God's divinity. Are you suggesting God doesn't have means to allow something like this to happen to Jacob?"

"Of course. I'm not denying it could have happened, it just feels beyond the scope of what God would normally do. Allowing a person to have full authority over their own world, to become God Himself. It all feels so absurd, even when compared to everything in the Bible.

"It's normal to question such a bold claim," Grace added, "Although it's a little ironic, Jacob apparently experiences a revelation from God Himself, yet our first instinct is to question whether or not it actually happened."

"Do you think it's wrong to question the authenticity of Jacob's revelation?"

"I don't think it's wrong to have some hesitations. You of all people should have some concern with blindly accepting everything you're told. But I don't understand why you're so stubborn when it comes to all of this."

"It's more than just simply accepting it," Pastor William confessed.

"Do you think accepting Jacob's story as true would cause you to abandon your own beliefs?" Grace persisted.

"I don't think that's the case. I think it has less to do with simply accepting his story as true, and more to do with the greater implications beyond the story itself."

"And what would that be?"

"If what Jacob wrote about is true and he discovered some apparent flaws in what I believe, then what else should I bring into question?"

Grace paused at her husband's admission of self doubt. Silence lingered for a moment before she inquired into the uncertainty dwelling within her husband's mind.

"Is there something else you think you should be questioning?"

"I don't know." the pastor confessed. "How do you feel about all of this? I know that you and I don't necessarily agree with each other when it comes to these sorts of subjects, but don't you have the same reservations I do?"

"I do," Grace admitted, while placing her empty spoon onto the table, "And while I'm still wrestling with everything myself, I'm beginning to think there may be more to God's design than what either of us believe."

"Do you think it's wrong that I don't want to abandon my beliefs?" Pastor William questioned.

"I don't think it's necessarily wrong, but limiting. Think about it, you used to believe that blindly accepting God's word was only scratching the surface of His depth, yet when someone has an apparent revelation from God himself, you have a hard time accepting it. Don't you see the irony in that?"

Pastor William tilted his head down as Grace's question increased the weight upon his mind.

"I don't know." his voice grew despondent in response to Grace's accusation.

"I know you well enough to know that if Jacob's writing was more in tune with your own belief you'd be more accepting of the revelation. You only began to doubt it because it doesn't adhere to what you believe to be true."

Grace's remark cut into the pastor's heart. "Well, don't *you* feel the same way?" Pastor William retorted, returning his focus to his wife. "Given what you've read so far I don't understand why you're not in the same position I'm in. We've had these discussions many times before, why only now do you appear to be more accepting of a different perspective?"

"It's not that I was denying your beliefs, or that I'm not having trouble accepting this." Grace defended herself, "It's just that your views have caused you to become a little stubborn when it comes to seeing another person's perspective."

"Do you think that my views don't allow for the freedom to accept other people's views of life?"

"Not in the way you've described it to me." Grace added, placing her spoon onto the table.

"What makes you say that?" he

questioned, having felt personally attacked.

"The way you see it, every choice, every decision comes down to God's predestination. It's limiting. Regardless of the question, your answer is God's will. With such a simple explanation, you'd only be scratching the surface of Jacob's revelation. Maybe if you become a little more open minded you might better understand what Jacob is trying to say."

"So you'd just like me to change my views on God's design for humanity?" he asked, feeling affronted.

"Listen, I'm not calling you to entirely abandon your beliefs, or to view Jacob's revelation as the absolute truth," Grace responded softly, attempting to simmer the debate between her and her husband, "I just think it might do you some good to calm down a little. That's all."

"I'll have to think about it," he remarked, recognizing the tone of Grace's voice and her desire to mitigate their disagreement from becoming a fight, "What about you though? You're suggesting I become more open minded, shouldn't you do the same?"

"Maybe once you show me you've become more open minded I'll follow suit." Grace said, before eating the last of her stew.

Their meal ended shortly after their conversation. The last remaining scraps of food were cleared from their bowls as the couple remained at their seats, attempting to calm down from their argument. With dinner over and the evening coming to a close, Pastor William excused himself from the kitchen table and began to make his way towards the seclusion of his bedroom.

The last remnants of the sunlight faded from the evening sky, marking the end of the day. Pastor William sat alone in seclusion while Grace occupied the living room and partook in her evening routine of watching the nightly newscasts; a routine she often shared with her husband so long as his attention wasn't focused elsewhere. Though the television was on, Grace's attention was distracted. In the calmness of the night, both the pastor and Grace reflected on their discussion. While Grace meditated on whether her accusations were authentic or based on her own feelings towards her husband's beliefs, Pastor William reflected on whether or not his pride prevented him from fully accepting Jacob's revelation.

In the stillness and tranquility of the coming dusk Pastor William began to pray. The silence and solitude of his bedroom provided him with the environment he needed to refocus his mind on God, seeking His wisdom in response to Grace's remarks. The silence of night continued to linger within the walls of their home as the couple's emotions began to settle.

Only once the distractions of the pastor's mind were removed could he once again begin to discern what God was speaking to him; or more specifically, what God was continuing to reveal to him in regards to Jacob's story. The pastor laid in his bed in silence, waiting in anticipation and faith that God would speak to him once again.

He waited for a word or revelation akin to the word of 'patience' he had received the night prior. He laid in solitude, waiting for God's 'voice'. A Bible rested atop his lap, opened in an effort for God to speak through His own divine written word. Alas, such a word or revelation never came to fruition. As the seconds turned to minutes the faith and optimism that God would speak to the pastor once more began to dwindle.

The pastor soon begrudgingly accepted that God's word wouldn't arrive that evening. He closed the Bible atop his lap and placed it on top of his nightstand. Switching off his bedside lap, the pastor extinguished the only remaining source of light within the room. As the darkness immediately cast over his body, Pastor William recited his nightly prayer before laying his head upon his pillow and drawing the bed sheets over himself.

The silence and seclusion Pastor

William dwelled within would quickly bring him to a deep state of slumber. He laid asleep, his body motionless, yet his mind continuing to process and think. Soon, either through his own efforts or through divine intervention, the answer he sought, the answer he prayed for, would be revealed in what he could only describe as a prophetic dream.

14

The pastor's eyes opened to a peculiar sight. An endless crowd of people gathered in a vast and open landscape. People of all races, old and young, sitting in silence. As his eyes passed over the sea of people he noticed their captivated expressions. Each and every person's attention was focused in a particular direction. As he reoriented his vision away from the crowd and closer to the source of their captivation, he inched ever closer to the purpose for their congregation. Despite his observation, Pastor William found himself at a loss as to the source of the crowd's attention, or the reason for their gathering.

Unable to ascertain the source of the crowds' focus, he decided to sit among them in their assembly. Despite his expectation, the stiffness in his body was absent, much to his relief. As he sat among the people, he began to hear the voice of a man, one that seemed to be far in the distance. As the pastor looked around, he could hear the voice draw ever closer to him, yet he was unable to discern the source of the sound.

Pastor William closed his eyes, severing his vision in hopes of placing his full attention on the voice projecting over the crowd. Eventually, the sound of the man's voice seemed to be within his reach. He opened his eyes once more to the sight of a man standing only a few feet before him. Despite having no recollection of who he was, Pastor William inexplicably knew the man's name; Joshua. He was dressed in robes of brown and white, appearing as though he was from a bygone era.

The tenderness of his expression and speech eased the uncertainty and confusion within the pastor's heart. Joshua seemed to exude wisdom beyond his years, despite physically appearing much younger than the pastor himself. There was a sense of familiarity in Joshua's presence, yet the pastor was unable to recognize any facet of him. He was a stranger, yet Pastor William was unable to deny the feeling that he knew Joshua, and that Joshua personally knew him. His words captivated the attention of the crowd, but his appearance was entirely unassuming.

The words Joshua spoke were in direct reference to the thoughts and concerns pressing upon the pastor's mind. He referenced and recited specific Biblical verses, as though he was a preacher giving a sermon from the Bible itself. The crowd was enamoured, hanging on his every word. And yet, as Pastor William turned his attention towards the preacher's face, he could see Joshua looking directly at him. Despite being a single person in an endless sea of faces, the pastor felt as though the preacher was speaking directly into his heart. The words he spoke carried a weight that humbled the storm dwelling within Pastor William's mind.

"Trust in the Lord with all your heart and lean not on your own understanding."

"The heart of man is deceitful above all things and desperately wicked."

Though the pastor had read those verses countless times over, after Joshua had audibly recited them they felt all the more tangible, all the more applicable and relevant to his circumstance. The preacher's words brought self-reflection into a situation the pastor had been entirely unwavering in. His voice didn't carry an accusatory tone, but one that gave credence to the doubts residing within Pastor William's heart since he had first read Jacob's revelation.

As the sermon progressed, Joshua's voice and tone began to subtly change. It no longer felt as though he was speaking directly into the pastor's heart, instead the preacher's focus shifted onto the endless crowd of people, as though his message was no longer meant for the pastor, but for the remainder of the congregation. With each successive word, Joshua's message became harder to comprehend. Yet despite the pastor's inability to understand his words, there was an unmistakable sense of reassurance arising within his heart.

Pastor William turned his attention towards the crowd once more. A boundless sense of joy and peace was spreading across the assembly of people. It appeared as though Joshua had spoken into the heart of each and every person, almost as though they were experiencing the same personal connection Pastor William had felt. As the pastor continued to gaze over the crowd, Joshua's voice began to fade. Pastor William turned his attention back towards Joshua, however to his surprise, the preacher had disappeared. His voice began to dissipate as it spread over the congregation, while his physical body had entirely vanished.

The crowd soon began to disperse. They arose from the ground and began to spread across the vast landscape, carrying within them the words Joshua had spoken into their hearts. As Pastor William watched the congregation dwindle, he soon found himself alone in the field. Joshua's words continued to resonate within the pastor's heart as he sat alone in silence. He understood that he too was to go forth into the world, armed with the wisdom Joshua had given; to trust not in his own understanding, but in the wisdom of his Heavenly Father. He closed his eyes once more, still meditating on the words he had heard while piecing together the answer he was given.

Pastor William awoke to the empty grey ceiling of his bedroom. He turned his head to his right side; laying next to him was Grace, fast asleep. The light of the morning sun shone through the window, contrasting the darkness cast into the bedroom hours earlier. The warmth of the rising sun spilled into the house as the stillness of the early morning marked the beginning of a new day. Pastor William laid awake in his bed, the slow repetition of Grace's breathing lulling him into a state of ease as he contemplated the dream he had awoken from.

He laid in silence, believing he had received the answer he sought. However he retained a faint hint of reluctance as the answer he received didn't align with the answer he had hoped for. The pastor turned to his wife once again, still sound asleep. Taking advantage of the morning silence, the pastor carefully crept out of his bed, desiring not to awaken Grace from her slumber, before making his way down the stairs towards the kitchen. He wanted to return Grace's favour from the previous morning and prepare breakfast for her while she lay asleep.

    He began to prepare the same breakfast Grace had provided him the morning prior. The aroma of the cooking eggs and frying bacon filled the air within his kitchen while he continued to discern the meaning behind his dream. The image of a man speaking to a crowd, reassuring them to trust not in their own understanding, but to have faith in God's wisdom and knowledge remained at the forefront of his thoughts. Either through divine intervention, or of his own subconscious, the pastor's dream spoke directly into the heart of the subject that was plaguing his mind. He wanted to simply reject the dream, but his mind remained fixated on the sight of the man and the crowd.

    Pastor William finished cooking while his mind continued to remain elsewhere. Turning the elements of the stove off, the pastor distributed the food onto two plates, grabbing hold of one and sitting down at the table. He decided against waking and inviting his wife to join him, mirroring the pastor's breakfast from the previous day. Sitting in silence, the pastor recited a habitual prayer before enjoying the fruits of his labour.

Pastor William remained in prayer throughout the duration of his breakfast. He was no longer praying for wisdom in discerning the meaning and validity of Jacob's revelation. Instead, he sought God's wisdom in relation to the dream he had awoken from. He reflected on the imagery of countless people heeding the message Joshua had spoken over them; going out into the vast world encouraged by the preacher's words. In the back of his mind he understood what was being spoken to him, yet he struggled to fully accept the direction he was given. In the silence his prayers transitioned from an internal dialogue into a vocal conversation with his Heavenly Father.

'God, I know You're speaking to me. I know Jacob gave me his story for a reason. I need You to strengthen me, to help me. I need to know what I'm supposed to do, who I'm supposed to reach out to, and who is in need of the revelation Jacob was blessed with. God, speak to me. Not for my sake, but for the sake of others. Reveal to me the path which I'm to follow for Your will to be done in my life, and in the lives of others. God, I want to be able to submit myself for Your plan and purpose, so You can touch the hearts of those who desire Your wisdom. You have a purpose and a plan for each of us. Lord, bring forth Your plan for our lives, and allow Your will to be done on Earth, as it is in Heaven.'

The pastor's prayers continued through his breakfast; for God to utilize Jacob's revelation to touch the hearts of those enduring the same emotional distress Jacob had experienced. As the time passed, the conclusion to both the pastor's prayers and his breakfast drew closer. He soon found himself emotionally, spiritually and physically satiated. With nothing left to pray, and an empty plate resting before him, he rose from his seat and began to clear the table, placing his now empty plate into the sink. Pastor William turned to the second plate of food on the counter top. Taking Grace's idea, the pastor located a pen and paper and quickly wrote a note to leave for his wife.

*I may not be as good a chef as you,
but I hope this will suffice.
-William*

With the meal concluded Pastor William cleaned and organized the kitchen. As he had finished cleaning, he suddenly recalled a request he had all but forgotten about. The guilt of his negligence ate at him as he climbed the stairs and entered into his study. He immediately grabbed hold of both a telephone and the letter resting atop a pile of sermon notes, cast aside when he first received Jacob's revelation. After briefly scanning over the letter to jog his memory, Pastor William began to recite the series of numbers written along the bottom of the letter, dialing each successive numeral into his phone in hopes of contacting the sender. The phone rang four times before being picked up.

"Hello, Michael?" Pastor William asked.

In the adjacent room Grace awoke to the smell of the breakfast her husband had prepared earlier that morning. Waking up to her husband's cooking was a rare occurrence, but was something she appreciated nonetheless. She laid awake, wanting to savour the moment and fragrance for a little longer before removing herself from the comfort of her bed and beginning her day.

She slowly climbed out of the sheets, before moving towards her wardrobe and deciding on her attire for the day. Her choice was of a simple white summer dress, one she had a particular fondness for, which gave her the appearance of an angel, at least according to her husband. Shortly after donning her dress and making her bed, Grace stepped outside of the bedroom; the same faint smell of breakfast grew stronger as she crossed over the threshold. The hallway darkened as Grace pulled the door closed, cutting off the natural morning light spilling in from the windows.

The door to Pastor William's study was closed. She refrained from knocking upon the door and potentially disturbing her husband to thank him for his culinary efforts that morning. Descending the staircase, she walked into the kitchen, which, much to her surprise and appreciation, was virtually spotless. Every piece of cookware had been washed and returned to its place within the cupboards, with the lone exception being a plate of food, a note and a pen left by her husband. She softly smiled while reading over the paper, before taking hold of the plate and walking towards the kitchen table.

Sitting down, Grace quickly blessed her food before thinking back to the conversation she had shared with her husband. As she ate, she reflected on Pastor William's unwillingness to change his belief, she began to wonder if she held the same reservations. Jacob's criticism of her own belief lingered in her mind, yet she desired to heed her own advice and open her mind to the new perspective that his revelation could provide.

However, despite her desire to become more open minded, her firmly held beliefs remained an ever present obstacle.

    Grace stood up from her seat, bringing with her the dishes she had eaten from just moments ago. She placed the plate and cutlery in the sink and began to run the water. A faint billow of steam steadily rose from the sink as she began to clean the last remnants of the breakfast. A tedious chore, yet one Grace found oddly relaxing, much to her husband's appreciation. The kitchen was once again clean, with the lone exception being the handwritten note Pastor William had left next to her plate. Grabbing hold of the pen, she wrote her reply directly beneath Pastor William's message.

    It was delicious. Thank you.

    Grace exited the kitchen, leaving behind the note for her husband before making her way back towards her bedroom. The ever present conversation of God's divinity and design for His children instilled a hunger within her to revisit God's written word. The dimly lit hallway at the top of the stairs began to fill with light as Grace opened the door to her bedroom.

    She entered into the room and retrieved her Bible from her nightstand while simultaneously basking in the warmth of the naturally illuminated room. She considered returning to the comfort of her bed to pray and study the Lord's word, however, she was entirely aware that if she were to rest atop the bed sheets she would not be arising until the mid afternoon.

Returning to the hallway, Grace made her way down the flight of stairs and into the living room. She sat down on the chesterfield, placed her Bible on her lap and began to flip through the pages until settling on the first gospel within the New Testament. The verses in the ninth chapter described the miraculous healing of a woman plagued with unending bleeding, who's healing was a result of her faith. The Biblical account of a miraculous restoration was not unlike that which Grace herself had experienced.

Similar verses and parables laid as the foundation of Grace's faith. The divine intervention she had experienced firsthand brought upon by her own submission and faith confirmed that God's influence was indeed possible. However, despite her own undeniable experience, the writings within Jacob's story continued to raise questions inside of her heart. To be told the absolute freedom Grace believed in would have in reality resulted in humanity's demise felt contrary to everything she had known.

For in Grace's eyes humanity's freedom brought God into their fallen world. It was through their prayers that God could bring healing and comfort to those who cried out to Him, and through God's freedom to heal did His presence become known. Alas, as Grace had reached the conclusion of Jacob's account of absolute free will, she began to question the validity of her beliefs. She wanted to remain steadfast in her belief, and yet she struggled to disregard all that she had read.

The absolute freedom that Grace believed in was brought into question as she indulged in the possibility that she was mistaken in her understanding of God and of humanity. She wanted to believe that humanity was in control of their own lives, yet she couldn't ignore the consequences that Jacob had described within his world. Grace desired to understand the truth behind Jacob's revelation, even if it set her on a path that would compromise the foundation of her beliefs. She reread the account of the woman who touched the hem of Jesus' robe. Through Grace's eyes, it was the woman's actions and faith that caused her healing, but through the eyes of her husband, the woman's healing was simply a result of God's predestination.

She continued to delve further into the Bible. Her prayers became more earnest with each successive verse. Like her husband, she attempted to discern the validity of Jacob's revelation through God's 'voice' and His word. Regardless of the amount of time she spent studying the Bible she felt unsatisfied. She couldn't shake the feeling that the answer she sought was hidden within Jacob's writing. In the room directly above Grace, Pastor William was concluding the phone call he had made following his breakfast that morning.

"It would be my honour. Again, thank you very much for the opportunity, Michael. I'll keep in contact with you until then. Goodbye." Pastor William said, before hanging up his phone.

He turned his attention to Jacob's writing resting atop his desk. Placing his fingertips onto the protruding bookmarks, he lifted the pages, revealing a single paper with two words written across the center: *'My Will'*. The criticism of predestination the pastor was wrestling with, and the answers he sought after remained hidden within the penultimate chapter of Jacob's story. He turned the paper over and scanned the handwritten wall of text before bringing his focus to the top of the page and beginning to read the story once more.

15

*

-My Will-

Control and freedom, peace and chaos. In my efforts to create a world fitting my own image of perfection I created a reality that was devoid of the true meaning of life and love. In my attempt at building a world in which absolute freedom was the cornerstone of humanity, I witnessed my creations fall into a depth of sin far greater than anything I could have anticipated. The feeling of inadequacy that I had endured throughout my life remained, despite now possessing the absolute omnipotence of a divine being.

I had the means to shape and alter reality on a whim, yet I still remained at a loss as to the cause of my previous failures. The power of God dwelled within me, yet despite forming and shaping billions of lives, I still lacked His wisdom. I desired to return to the moment of creation once more; to create a world in which my design and plan for humanity could exist simultaneously with freedom, and consequently, with chaos and sin.

The limitless potential of each and every individual laid before me; the blank canvas I had observed previously was mine to command once again. While I could control the lives of my creations, I desired their sentience above all else. I wanted to find the balance between two polar opposites, two differing aspects of reality; free will and predestination. Merging two conflicting ideals felt insurmountable, and yet through my omnipotence I knew that such a feat was entirely feasible.

As I gazed into the blank slate of humanity's infinite possibilities, I reflected upon the timeline of my creations' lives when given freedom and consciousness. The near infinite outcomes for humanity was a direct result of their sentience, yet not entirely of their own volition. Though my creations possessed the freedom to decide their actions, certain opportunities could only arise through the actions of another. As I reflected upon the arduous task of combining my creation's freedom and my control, I meditated on my own understanding and the wisdom of The Man who presided over me.

"How am I supposed to make sense of all of this?" I asked.

"What is it that you are specifically seeking?" The Man responded.

"That's just it, I don't really know." Waves of uncertainty and confusion bombarded my mind, "I want to make a world where my people can freely choose their lives, but I don't want to see them suffer again."

"You desire to control their lives, and for them to control themselves. You have an interest in their well being, yet you do not want to bless them with a world of eternal perfection. Reflect upon this; what is it that you're asking of Me?"

I paused for a brief moment at The Man's unexpected question. "I want to know what I'm missing." I finally replied

"The answer you seek is one you've sought countless times in your life." He alluded, "Reflect upon your prayers, what did you continually seek?"

I looked back on my cries to God; prayers for healing during my moments of emotional anguish, prayers to understand the life I had lived and the struggles I had endured, and for wisdom in discerning God's will and direction for my life.

"I prayed to know why my life was so unfair," I recalled, *"And to know what path God had intended for me."*

"Do you believe that it's possible for there to be both a predetermined plan, and free will?"

The Man's question perplexed me. Despite possessing the omnipotence to shape reality with a single thought, I remained uncertain of how I could allow such conflicting possibilities to coexist.

"I don't know. I don't understand how I can combine their free will with my desire for their lives. How am I supposed to make sense of this?"

"Reflect upon your own understanding and knowledge of life. You already possess the answer that you seek."

I gazed upon the inhabitants of my world, meditating on all that I'd learned up until that moment, my experiences and failures in creating two worlds, one solely predicated upon predestination, the other predicated upon absolute freedom.

"How can You be so sure I already know the answer?"

"I know your heart and mind. I can see your understanding and the knowledge that dwells within it. Take hold of it, for it shall reveal to you the revelation you seek."

"What if I can't do it?" I lamented, "What if I mess up again and make everything worse?"

"You are the alpha and the omega, the beginning and the end of your reality. You hold time within your hands. Trust not in your own understanding, but in the faith I have in you."

I understood what I had to do. I understood what The Man was asking of me, and the actions I had to take to fully understand the revelation I was experiencing. Looking upon my creations, I once again began to orchestrate a plan for the entirety of humanity, one intricately woven for each individual being. Their lives connected and intertwined with one another. Their paths flowed and intersected; merged and separated. A singular decision could set the groundwork for a lifetime of potential opportunities. A single mistake could result in years of unending struggles.

A near infinite series of paths lay before each person. Yet at the center of it all, at the foundation of humanity's potential, laid my desires for each and every being; my will for their lives. Not as the singular path I had initially believed to be God's design for His children, but instead as a series of opportunities. Through their freedom they could experience one of many paths I had intended for their lives. While all paths were of my design, not every path followed my will. Though the path to follow my will was narrow there still existed choices within the limitations. By seeking and following my paths, my creations could experience a different, yet equally fulfilling life. Just as the paths for their lives were vast, so too were their opportunities to follow my will.

A lifetime of choices were given in an instant. A complex series of unactualized potential laid before each and every person. At the center of their lives stood the capacity for freedom and for choice. Each point, each moment in their lives, allowed for different opportunities. Underlying every choice, every opportunity, stood my desire for their lives.

As I gazed upon my creation's lives and the paths I laid out for them, I began to dwell upon the life I had lived leading up to this very moment. Throughout my life I continually sought to understand the path that God had designed for me. Though my prayers remained unanswered, God provided me with some semblance of knowledge that I was wilfully abandoning His direction for my life. Although He still allowed me the sentience to follow a path of my choosing, unfortunately as a consequence of my freedom to ignore God's plan for my life I found myself falling deeper into depths of nihilism and depression. Even though I lamented on the thought of allowing my creations to succumb to the darkness of sin once again, I could find solace in knowing there existed a divine plan for each of their lives.

Mirroring the freedom God had instilled within myself and the rest of humanity, my creations possessed the sentience to follow a path of their own volition. However, each opportunity and diverging path was laid by my own design. Every decision had a consequence, and every choice had a different outcome. Every path I had laid before humanity was filled with joy and peace, trials and tribulations, pain and sorrow. The consequences of their choices arose a myriad of emotions and experiences

Despite the inevitable pain and sorrow that existed in every path for their lives, the greatest satisfaction and fulfillment they could experience was only possible through following my will. They understood their own desires, but through my omniscience I understood their potential.

In order for my creations to know my path for their lives they first had to know me. At the initial stages of creation I began to bestow humanity with a revelation; one of my own existence. While the revelation my creations experienced differed from the Biblical accounts of a prophetic messiah, or the retelling of historical events, the descriptions of God's interactions with His children mirrored that of my own interactions with my creations.

Small ideas birthed through philosophical thoughts would lead my creations down a path of spiritual discovery. The innate desire of purpose and meaning within every person's heart instilled a yearning to look beyond their senses, seeking the reason for their existence and ultimately finding me. Through their prayers I began to speak to a small fraction of my creations; an elected, whom I had preordained with the potential to document my existence. While some of those whom I elected would willingly ignore my calls, others became the arbiters of my word and law.

Those who heeded my calls provided the world with a tangible account of my presence, and a discernible moral law which my creations could adhere to, or deny. While my physical presence remained beyond their senses, my essence and word became accessible. Despite my creations having some knowledge of my existence, I still allowed for them to retain a level of uncertainty in order to preserve their freedom.

I remained above and beyond time, reflecting upon the infinite complexity of each person's life. While they possessed the freedom to willingly follow the paths of my design, they also had the freedom to defile their morality and indulge in the sin and darkness of their world. Despite the potential for my creations to allow sin to consume their lives, the faith in my word and in my existence held by not only those I had elected, but all those who sought my divinity ushered in a light to cast away the encroaching darkness.

Through their faith they could discern my desires for their lives. They could experience the comfort and reassurance in knowing I had ordained a purpose and reason for their existence. However just as my relationship with God didn't release me from my emotional distress, my creation's faith wasn't a means to absolve them of the pain and darkness encompassing their world. Instead, their relationship with me strengthened their hope and resolve despite the surrounding sin.

Their entire timeline was on full display before me. While the all encompassing darkness I previously witnessed had yet to be entirely extinguished, its presence was nothing more than a faint shadow. While the consequences of sin still rippled into their physical world, the resulting pain was nothing more than a fraction of what I had previously witnessed.

The small fragments of sin that still

remained were simply a result of my creation's freedom to deny my existence and allow the darkness within their hearts to grow. However, the light brought upon by those who sought my presence all but cleansed the sin gripping the world. The concern that enveloped my heart began to recede, easing my worries and confirmed in myself the faith The Man had in me.

Despite my creations knowing of my word and following my paths, I once again began to hear their cries. Their prayers were not solely to understand my will, but also for comfort in their darker circumstances, reality they existed within was rife with pain and sorrow. In their freedom they could experience the emotional distress from loss and heartbreak. Though they viewed their pain as unjust, through my omniscience I could witness the full reality of their circumstances.

Unbeknownst to my creations, the paths I had designed for them frequently required their submission and faith in me. The pain they endured was often a result of their own stubbornness as they held onto their own desires while attempting to follow my will. The anxiety that so many experienced was brought upon by a reluctance to endure a temporary moment of patience I asked of them. Ignoring my directions in lieu of following their own selfishness inevitably led my creations down a path of emotional strain and distress. However, by trusting my will, their joy and peace would eclipse the emotional strain they had once endured.

Above all else, the inability of some to have faith in my timing, and their hesitation in seeking my desire for their lives consequently led them down the same path of depression I had previously walked myself. Though the pain in following my desires initially felt overwhelming, the blessings my creations would receive for their faith and submission always exceeded their greatest expectations.

Through my omniscience I could see both into my creations' hearts and into their futures. I could see their intentions and I could witness the ramifications of my intervention. Their perspective was limited, lacking the full foresight that I was able to observe. While the consequences of my actions may have been immediately satisfying, it would deny them of the plans I intended for them.

I began to reflect on my own life leading up to that point. The emotional strain my creations endured, and the understanding and release they cried out for mirrored my life in more ways than one. However, it was during these moments that I was able to see a reality beyond my initial perspective; a glimpse into the perspective God had of my life. Though my suffering and depression was a consequence of my lack of faith in God's timing, it was through my distress that God had allowed me to reach a point of absolute helplessness, in order for me to willingly submit myself for His purposes.

During my life I had always believed I was seeking God's will, yet I was unable to relinquish the trust I had in myself instead of placing it in God. Only by seeing the world through His eyes did I begin to understand the realities of my life and why it continually felt unfair and unjust. I always felt as though God was ignoring my cries, however, in reality, it was me who refused to trust in God's will and timing, ultimately following my own path instead of the one God had desired for me to follow; a divine plan, absent of the depression and nihilism I had endured. While I don't believe that God had intended me to experience my depression, it was through my pain that He began to speak to me.

The pain and loss I had experienced brought me to a point of greater revelation than I could have ever known; a point that God not only allowed me to reach, but also one He had intended for me. He required me to relinquish my growing anger and nihilism, and to cry out to Him. However, only by initially desiring His will, and trusting that He had an intended purpose for my life, could I have reached this very moment of divine revelation.

I began to understand that while God had an intended revelation for me, it could only be actualized through a loss greater than anything I could have anticipated. Though Alexander's life and death initially seemed unjust, as I witnessed humanity through divine eyes, I could see not only the boundless joy those like him brought into the lives of so many, but I could also witness the joy and happiness that existed within the lives of those like Alexander. However in humanity's limited perspective, when witnessing those like Alexander we would all instinctually pray for God's intervention and restoration. Yet from God's perspective, such a healing would only deny humanity of His will for their lives, ultimately limiting the full extent of God's blessings.

Though my family and I continually prayed for God's will to be done in all of our lives, they were not prepared for the realities of God's will, for it can often appear darker and more painful than we would expect. Just as my creations' pain could serve a greater purpose, so too did my family's loss serve a purpose beyond our understanding. Yet it was through our loss that I received this revelation; a revelation with the means to bring reassurance and comfort in the midst of a dark storm.

As I gazed upon the inhabitants of my world, I could see the darkness of sin within all of humanity, including those who diligently followed my paths. Despite attempting to remove themselves from the sin of their world and live within my divine light, each person's heart housed the same darkness that had once suffocated my world.

"Why is this happening?" I asked, "Why is the darkness still there?"

"It is their inherent nature." The Man responded, "The capacity to sin, the potential to disobey your intention for them is a part of their very essence."

"I don't get it. Why is there some sinful nature in them if I never put it there in the first place?"

"For as the Bible says, 'Man was made in the image of God', so too were your creations made in your image. While man fell after his creation, your creations have fallen because of you. Despite the divinity you possess, your very nature is marred with the sin of humanity's fall, and their darkness reflects the darkness within your own heart."

"Is it possible for me to remove it?"

"Yes, but in doing so you'd be altering their very nature and removing their free will, returning your world to its first state of existence. Your intention was to endow your creations with the capacity to follow their own

desire. The sinful nature they inherited from your image grants them the potential to indulge in the very sin that you are capable of committing yourself."

"Is there anything I can do to remove their sin without changing their nature?"

"Yes, the most important blessing one can bestow upon another; forgiveness. For in God's endless mercy, humanity's sins were removed. So too can your creations' sins be removed through your own forgiveness."

"How is that supposed to work? I mean, in the Bible Jesus died on a cross for our sins, but I don't have a son to die for my creations."

"The blood of Jesus was necessary to absolve the sinful nature of humanity so they could be viewed as blameless in the eyes of their Heavenly Father. However, through the eyes of a divine creator possessing his own sinful nature, such a sacrifice is not needed. Simply pardoning their sins and forgiving them of their transgressions is all that's required for you to see them as spotless."

"How does my forgiveness remove their darkness and sin?" I asked, gazing at the faint darkness that continued to linger in my world and my creations.

"The darkness you see is the physical embodiment of their sin, and by forgiving them, the darkness shall dissipate. Though

their actions often violate your morality, through your mercy they are no longer bound to the sin that grips their world. They are no longer seen as sinful, but spotless in your eyes. Beyond your own forgiveness, you must also instruct your creations to forgive one another just as you have forgiven them. For while your forgiveness removes their sins from your eyes, only when your creations' sins are removed from their own eyes will the darkness truly begin to disappear from your world."

"I have to ask, what are the consequences of their sin?" I asked, "I've heard countless times that Jesus' death saves us from the punishment of sin and brings us to Heaven once we die, but I didn't create a Heaven or Hell for my creations. What actually happens to them when they die?"

"For without your own creation of a Heaven and Hell, in their death they simply cease to exist, remaining as nothing more than a fleeting memory in the minds of the rest of your creations."

"If that's the case and my forgiveness doesn't actually prevent them from going to Hell, then why is my forgiveness necessary?"

"Look upon the world once more."

I returned my attention to my creations, seeing the guilt and pain still present in their lives and the darkness consuming their hearts and souls.

"Listen to their prayers and hear their cries. Within your own heart, begin to forgive them of their sins and transgressions. Absolve them of the growing guilt within their hearts, and release them of the blight of darkness gripping their souls."

The empathy in my heart grew as I heard their cries.

"Now, forgive them as you have forgiven your own transgressors. Let go of their disobedience, and embrace them as a father embraces his own children."

Within an instant I could feel the pain and cries of those who followed my will and moral laws, and sought after my mercy begin to fade. The emotional storm and guilt within their hearts and minds disappeared in an instant. The darkness within their lives had been erased, leaving their hearts and souls as spotless, yet my questions remained ever present.

"How did this happen? Why did this happen?" I asked.

"Their sins were the result of their disobedience in following your will, your morals and your path for their lives; as is the very nature of sin. The moment you forgave them of their sins, their pain was resolved. You no longer remember their sins, and in your forgiveness you absolved them of their pain and guilt."

I looked upon my world in amazement at how a simple act of forgiveness allowed my creations to be released of their pain and sorrow.

"What am I supposed to do now?" I asked.

"Listen."

I heeded His word and listened to the thoughts and voices of my creations. A torrent of praise and joy flooded into my mind. The release of their pain and sorrow caused an outpour of thankfulness in response to my forgiveness. Those who experienced my forgiveness and mercy were no longer bound by the guilt of sin, but delighted in the agape love I had shown towards them.

Those whose faith had begun to dwindle gained a renewed strength and optimism as they expectantly awaited for answers to their prayers. Those who denied my will and mercy gained a growing fascination and intrigue towards my potential existence; one born out of witnessing the boundless joy and peace that existed within the lives of those who received my forgiveness. As a result of my forgiveness and the agape love that existed between myself and those who accepted my divinity, my creations began to evangelize my existence, ultimately bringing all of my creation closer to my presence.

Amidst my creations' joy I could feel a growing appreciation beyond anything I had known. As a result of their freedom from sin, I could experience the depth of love that humanity felt towards their Heavenly Father, and the extent to which God would go to allow man to know of His presence. Though my presence was accessible to all of my creations, only those who knew of their sins and sought my forgiveness could experience the true extent of my love and mercy.

I looked upon the world once more. In my creations' freedom they were able to decide their own paths and destiny. Yet as my presence became more prominent in their lives, their willingness to seek my will grew stronger. As humanity's sin began to fade through my forgiveness, so too did the darkness and calamities begin to disappear from the world. As my mercy steadily spread throughout the lives of my creations, the frequent natural disasters and sicknesses that had plagued my creations began to dwindle. However, just as my creations' fallen nature remained an intrinsic part of their essence, so too did the sicknesses and disasters remain a part of their world.

In my initial efforts to manifest a perfect world through predestination I brought forth a world that was devoid of genuine love. In my attempt to create a world of absolute freedom I caused chaos and the darkness of sin to consume and destroy my creations. Only after I allowed my creations to willingly choose or deny my will and preordained plans, did I create a world that truly felt complete.

In those final moments I began to fully understand the revelation God had intended for me. In order to grasp the depth of His love and forgiveness, I had to see the world through the lens of its creator. Then and only then could I begin to understand the true depth of God's wisdom and logic.
"I think I get it now, I think I finally understand what I was missing."

"Good." The Man replied, "Now there is one request I have for you." He then began to speak the same indecipherable language I had heard twice before.

Within a matter of seconds the endless ocean of stars and galaxies began to disappear. The world before me began to fade, returning to the void from which it originated. As the distance between the creator and the created grew, so too did the concern in my heart for their lives. Despite witnessing my creations fade from my sight, an unmistakable sense of calmness came over me.

"Worry not, for they are in my care." The Man reassured me.

There was an unspoken understanding

that despite my lack of presence in and above their world, the beings that I had created were in the same hands of The Man who had given me this revelation of divinity, purpose and faith. The darkness soon overtook my sight as I began to feel myself returning to my physical body. The warmth of the air touched my skin as the light of the sunless sky shone through my eyelids. Opening my eyes, I gazed upon the vast and beautiful landscape once more before returning my focus to The Man standing before me.

*

16

Pastor William was at a loss for words. He raised his head from the pages before him, while attempting to mitigate the uncertainty in his mind. The questions he'd been wrestling with, the doubts that had been plaguing his mind for the past two days had been answered, yet the conclusion Jacob reached felt so contrary to what he had expected. He wanted to retain his aforementioned beliefs in God's design for humanity. However, the grip he once firmly held on his beliefs had begun to wane. The revelation Jacob gave him had planted a seed in the pastor's heart and mind that had the potential to upend the foundation of his understanding.

He had reached a crossroads, to either continue to hold onto his long held beliefs, or instead to accept that his understanding of God's nature was, at best, incomplete. Time passed slowly as he weighed each option in his mind. Every argument that he had once accepted felt insufficient in light of everything he had read.

Pastor William scanned the paragraphs once more before inserting his bookmark and moving the booklet to the side of his desk. Despite wanting to spend the rest of his time reading through Jacob's story, another commitment took precedence at that moment. With the surface of his desk clear, the pastor opened one of the drawers to this right, before grabbing hold of a pencil and a small notepad.

The remainder of the afternoon was spent constructing a short speech for the wedding he was asked to officiate. Given his job and title of 'Pastor', he was well acquainted with the art of public speaking, however the responsibility of officiating a wedding instilled in him a sense of nervousness he rarely experienced. Though the honour of marrying a couple had been bestowed on him from time to time throughout the duration of his adult life, his nerves would always remain present until the wedding had concluded.

The sound of the pencil scratching

against the paper was all that could be heard within the walls of the pastor's study. Minutes passed as the pages began to fill. He drafted his speech, yet the majority of attention was directed elsewhere. Lingering thoughts of the uncertainty continuing to echo in his mind as he places his words onto the papers. While the pastor tended to his responsibilities by constructing his speech, he attempted to distract and distance himself from the thoughts swirling in his mind. However, despite his efforts he soon found himself lost within his own mind once more; attempting to rationalize what it was he believed to be true of God's design for humanity.

    The stiffness in the pastor's antiquated body grew as the late afternoon drew closer. Needing to stretch his body, he arose from his chair and began to make his way towards the door. He exited his study and entered into his bedroom before changing from his nightly attire into a more casual outfit. Dressing himself in a plaid button-down shirt and grey slacks, the pastor walked out of his bedroom and into the hallway. Standing at the top of the flight of stairs, he saw Grace walk from the living room to the kitchen. Despite his attempt to subtly descend the staircase, Grace immediately recognized the sound of her husband's footsteps.

    "I wasn't sure if I was going to see you

at all today." Grace remarked, her back turned towards him.

"That's entirely up to you I suppose." Pastor William quipped, looking at his wife's back.

"Don't give me any ideas," she teased, mirroring her husband's cadence.

Pastor William smiled at his wife's witticism.

"I'm actually surprised you decided to venture out of your room a second time today," Grace remarked, pointing at the note her husband had left out earlier that morning. His wife's handwriting beneath his own caught his attention.

It was delicious. Thank you.

"You've put up with me being cooped up in my study for most of the week. It's the least I can do."

"I do really appreciate it. Just don't keep this going on for too long, it's starting to get boring not seeing you around here."

"Don't worry, I'm just about done."

"That's good." she replied,"Anyway, are you planning on sticking around down here, or are you going to lock yourself up in your chambers again?"

"I'd actually prefer to take a bit of a break and try to clear my mind. I read a little more into the story, but I think I'll need some time to process it all before I return to it."

"I'm glad to hear that," she replied, as she turned towards her husband. "I wouldn't mind reading a little more of it now that you've finally decided to take a break."

"I'll be returning to the church tomorrow, you can use that time to catch up."

"If you're not preoccupied with your story is there anything you'd like to do this afternoon?"

"There is actually one thing you might be able to assist me with."

"Oh, and what would that be?" Grace inquired.

The pastor waved his hand over to the kitchen table, "Take a seat."

A majority of the pastor's knowledge of weddings was fuelled by Grace's passion towards the sacred event. The couple sat down as Pastor William discussed his request to officiate the upcoming wedding while Grace assisted him in writing his officiant speech. Despite his experience officiating weddings, Pastor William always sought Grace's humour and wit in compiling his speeches.

The couple spent the remainder of the afternoon going over Pastor William's responsibilities for the upcoming day. While he had initially used the wedding to distance himself from Jacob's story, he enjoyed watching Grace indulge in one of her deepest passions. Minutes turned to hours as Grace continued to discuss her own ideas for the ceremony, though she wouldn't be in attendance. Her passion and eagerness towards the subject soon overtook the conversation, energizing her, while exhausting her husband.

Pastor William watched the sun set through the kitchen window as Grace continued to digress. A blanket of darkness soon spread across the sky as the sun crept beneath the horizon, marking the end of the day. The conversation the couple shared had all but silenced the internal dialogue echoing within the pastor's mind. As their banter slowed down and the calmness of night set in, an audible growl from the pastor's stomach caught Grace's attention.

"Excuse me," The pastor muttered.

Grace flashed a cheeky smile at her husband, "I think it's time for me to repay you for breakfast."

She stood up from her chair and walked towards the refrigerator. "I'll be a few minutes, you should go over your speech in the meantime."

Grace removed the remnants of the leftover stew from the fridge and placed it onto the stove top as the pastor finished reading over his script. Pastor William closed his notepad just as Grace placed two bowls of stew onto their kitchen table. Joining her husband, Grace sat down and quickly prayed over their food.

Casual small talk shared between a husband and his wife filled their house as the couple conversed over their dinner. The aforementioned topic of weddings brought forth memories of their own walk down the aisle. The couple fondly reminisced about the day Pastor William had taken Grace's hand in marriage; a day filled with joy and tears, a day so distant in the past, yet recalled as though it was only the day before last. The tenderness of their conversation and the retelling of their own wedding carried over to the late evening, until the moment the couple retired to their bedroom.

The moon traversed the night sky, rising and setting across the horizon. The sun soon travelled a similar path, bringing forth the dawn of a new day. As the morning began so too did Pastor William's day. Rising from his bed he would soon depart from his home and return to the responsibilities of the church building that he dearly missed.

Grace's day began shortly after her husband left their home as she awoke to the stillness and silence of an empty household. Arising from her bed, she made her way into the hallway outside of the bedroom. Directly in front of her was her husband's study; the door wide open, displaying the cluttered mess he had yet to touch, much to her dismay. Resting among the disarray was the booklet that remained the focal point of Grace and the pastor's attention. Heeding her husband's advice, Grace overlooked the disorganized state of his study and grabbed hold of the booklet titled *'My Story'*. She decided against returning to the comfort of her bed to indulge in Jacob's writing, opting for the living room chesterfield instead.

Craving a cup of tea, Grace stopped off in the kitchen before making her way to the living room. She stood in front of the kitchen counter where an empty mug and full kettle sat before her. She casually flipped through the pages of Jacob's writing whilst waiting for the water inside the kettle to boil. As the steam began to rise from the kettle, Grace turned her attention away from the papers in her hand and towards the empty mug. After filling her cup Grace grabbed a single teabag from the kitchen cupboard and placed it inside its bath to steep.

Firmly gripping the papers in her left hand and the tea in her right, Grace made her way into the living room, sat down on the chesterfield and took a small sip of tea before returning her attention back to Jacob's story. She once again flipped through the pages before reaching her white bookmark resting above the words *'My Will'*. Lifting the bookmark from the pages and placing it atop her lap, she began to read Jacob's account of creating a divine plan within a reality of sentience.

    At that same moment, Pastor William sat down in front of his desk and began to outline his intended sermon. While he had initially planned to utilize aspects of Jacob's revelation in his message, he remained uncertain if his original message coincided with his current beliefs. Throughout their afternoon, both the pastor and his wife's ideas were continually challenged. Each one attempted to reject their doubts, yet their uncertainty remained ever present.

    After consuming the last of her tea, Grace leaned over and placed the empty cup on the table before her. She then turned her eyes to the virtually empty page resting on her lap. Written against a white background was a single word, a word both symbolic of the final chapter and the culmination of the story; *'Revelation'*. Turning the page over she began her final delve into Jacob's story.

17

*

-Revelation-

My eyes remained fixated on The Man standing before me.
"There is much I need to discuss with you, and much more you need to understand. Please come with Me." He beckoned, stretching out His hand towards me.
I took hold of His wrist. There was a near weightlessness to me as He raised me to my feet. The Man stood in front of me; a welcoming smiling covered His face, as though He had been patiently waiting for me to awaken from my slumber. At that moment the same influx of peace that I had initially felt when I first awoke in the meadow completely

covered me, calming my disbelief and reassuring me of the validity and reality of my experience. I was speechless in that moment, at odds as to how I could comprehend something so inexplicable, yet so tangible. The Man walked past me and descended the hill we were perched atop. I remained standing in hesitation before returning to my senses.

"What was that?" I asked, steadily catching up to The Man in front of me.

"That which you have just experienced is the very same answer you seek, and the answer that so many like you are still in need of."

"What was it though?" I asked, "Was it some sort of dream, or did it really happen?"

"Does the legitimacy of a revelation require the experience to be authentic?"

"What do You mean?" I questioned as I walked shoulder to shoulder with The Man.

"Regardless of whether your experience was real, or a simple dream, that doesn't negate the validity of your revelation, and the knowledge you've gained."

"But I still don't fully understand what happened."

"What is it that you're still trying to grasp?"

"Why am I only learning all of this now?" I turned my head towards The Man, "I

mean, I know that I'm not the only one who thought life was unfair. I kept praying for an answer, but why did it have to happen only after Alexander died?"

"The revelation could have happened regardless, but the depth of your revelation and understanding is correlated with your circumstances. For only those dwelling in the true depths of darkness are willing to fully cast away themselves and cry out to their Heavenly Father." He turned His attention towards the sunless sky, "You must remember, when seeking your Heavenly Father's will, you're wilfully submitting your own freedom in faith that His plans for your life are greater than your own. You continually prayed for direction in your life, yet when circumstances felt as though they were beyond your control, you assumed that it was no longer in His control either. Just as man cannot serve two masters, you cannot pursue both your own desires and your Heavenly Father's."

"Is it possible for me to follow both His plans for my life and my own plans?" I asked, while The Man's attention was still turned towards the open sky.

"There may be times both paths intersect, but to fully follow His plan, you must be willing to relinquish your own freedom. Though you may endure pain and turmoil, by following the will of your

Heavenly Father, such moments of sombreness can often bring forth greater opportunities that may only be caused through loss or pain. Following His will doesn't mean you'll be absolved of pain. Instead, it is trusting that there's purpose and reason for such pain to exist. This I know you've already begun to understand."

"I know that, but now what? Did all of this happen just so that I can find some sort of comfort in my life?

"No," He answered, turning towards me, "The understanding you've received is for a purpose far greater than yourself. The same prayers you've cried have echoed throughout history. The knowledge and wisdom you've received is as much for yourself as it is for others."

"So what am I supposed to do?"

My question lingered as The Man stopped walking. It was at that moment I realized our conversation had carried the two of us back to the edge of the river at which we had met. The stillness and tranquility of the atmosphere mirrored the moment when I first awoke in the meadow. The birds and fish I had seen before gathered near The Man once again as He approached the base of the waterfall. The Man looked down towards the small school of fish before sitting down and gesturing to me to do the same.

"Just as your experience gave you greater insight into your own life, so too should you use your experience to speak to those whose lives are equally marred with darkness and depression."

"And how am I supposed to speak to them?"

"Have faith. If you truly desire to follow your Heavenly Father's will, you'll find the means to do just that. Don't place the Lord within your own limitations, but submit yourself and you shall receive direction."

The gentle sound of the waterfall rested in the air as I began to meditate upon what The Man said, and the opportunity I was given. I knew that even the most fervent and faithful believers would find hesitation in fully accepting all that I had experienced. While I understood that I was endowed with the potential to speak to those who struggled as I did, I was also aware of the division that could arise within various sects of the Christian faith. There was no question as to what I was being called to do, however, my resolve began to wane as I further contemplated what The Man was asking of me.

"I have to ask, why me? I mean, so many have gone through the same, or worse than I have, yet I'm the one who was picked to answer all their questions? Why was I chosen

over others, can't other people receive their own revelation?"

"Your struggle is familiar to so many, and for that very same reason your story will speak to those in need. While they may initially question the role they play in a divine plan, only after their journey is complete do they understand the logic of their Heavenly Father's decision and why they were chosen. Hindsight can often provide the greatest comfort."

I meditated on The Man's answer while gazing at the school of fish before me.

"How am I even supposed to get started?"

"Plant a single seed. Just as the smallest mustard seed has the potential to grow into a mighty and magnificent tree, so too do you possess the means to speak to those beyond your vision. Begin the journey and your path shall be known."

"So I just need to talk to someone?" I asked, gazing at The Man's reflection in the flowing river, "What if they don't believe me?"

"Belief or disbelief rests with them. You simply need to speak to those who are willing to listen. Their hearts will resonate with yours, and their ears will hear your message regardless of their own knowledge or understanding. Your calling is not towards

evangelism, but to provide an explanation for those who are enduring circumstances not unlike your own."

"I get that." I replied, still trying to come to grips with everything. "Even though I know what you're asking me, I still have some doubts in whether or not this is actually happening."

"Having faith in a God you cannot see is difficult. Even those who have experienced divine intervention can often express doubt. However, despite their doubt, they still hold onto their faith. For it is in their faith that the Lord's path becomes real."

"Is it wrong that I'm struggling to have faith, even with everything that just happened?"

"Every day, people reach a crossroads; a choice to continue to hold onto their faith, or to abandon it. While some have greater faith than others, all experience doubt. While the Lord speaks to many, only those with faith seek Him."

"I think I understand, but what am I supposed to do now?"

"Walk out in faith. Trust in the plans of your Heavenly Father, for He will not leave you, nor forsake you."

"What about You? What are You going to do?"

"Just as a good shepherd must tend to

his flock, I too must tend to My sheep. So many are crying out, entirely unaware that the answer they seek is approaching."

"Am I the first person to experience all of this?" I asked, turning my head towards The Man, who was still gazing upon the fish gathered at the edge of the river, "I've never heard of anything even coming close to this, but that doesn't mean that something like this hasn't happened before, right?"

"While many have reached their own revelations, their journeys were different than yours." He answered, "Each person requires a revelation unique to themselves. Each revelation serves a purpose, and each person walks a distinct path. The underlying divinity transcends each individual plan, yet the path they walk differs."

"So have others been here before?"

"Some have walked with Me in this paradise."

I began to look around, taking in the breathtaking scenery once more.

"Will I ever return?"

"Perhaps one day. However, it is better for you to find comfort and solace in your faith, than for you to return here once more."

"I think You're right," I said as our conversation came to a close.

I wanted to continue to dwell in that moment, to continue to converse with The

Man. However, despite my desires, I understood that my reason for arriving in that meadow had been fulfilled, and that my time with The Man had reached its conclusion. A final moment of silence passed as I resided in the beauty of the immaculate scenery. I was hesitant to leave, lamenting the moment of my departure, but I knew it was time nonetheless.

I arose from the ground and began to walk away, uncertain as to where I was heading, or when I'd reach my destination, but I knew that I would arrive regardless. I followed the river once more, walking alongside its slow current. As I traversed the river's edge, I turned around to The Man, to thank him for all that He had done, yet to my surprise He was nowhere to be seen. Despite finding myself alone in the meadow, I didn't feel as though I was abandoned. The Man was gone, yet His presence lingered both around and within me.

As I followed the river's current I began to pray. My prayers were no longer focused on my own dark circumstances, instead, my focus was on the plans and purposes God had for my life. Just as I had done countless times before, I began to pray, yet for the first time I felt as though God was truly listening. The feeling of praying into a void had been replaced with an unmistakable

sense that my Heavenly Father was truly with

me in that moment.

"God, I'm sorry for my anger towards You. For so long I felt as though You didn't care about me. It always felt as though no matter how much I prayed to You, You were just ignoring me, leaving me behind for the sake of everyone else. But after all of this I don't think that was Your intention at all. You were listening. You were guiding me to walk Your path for my life.

"But I refused to step out in faith. I spent so long holding onto my resentment and anger that I couldn't trust You. Now I'm beginning to understand that Your plan for my life requires me to let go of myself and place my faith in You. Although I often prayed for Your intervention in my life, only after Alexander died was I able to truly abandon myself and reach out to You.

"I know that if I had walked alongside Julia, or my friends I wouldn't have found myself here. I know that if all my prayers were answered, there'd be no reason for me to seek You anymore. Only now I know that in order for You to reveal Yourself to me, I needed to be willing to hear you; I needed to reach the point where I had nothing left but faith. Only then could I receive Your revelation. Though I once felt abandoned, only now I understand how You were orchestrating my life. Lord,

continue to guide me. Continue to reveal Your

path for my life and replace my desire with Yours. Allow Your will to be done in my life, as You see fit."

My prayers continued as I walked along the river's current; prayers rooted in self reflection and a desire to submit my life for God's purposes. It was then that I shifted my focus away from my life and realigned it on my relationship with my Heavenly Father. As I continued walking, either through pure coincidence or through divine direction, I returned to a familiar location within the meadow. Though I had remained focused on my prayers, I found myself in the same open expanse where I had first awakened. I concluded my prayers, having traversed an endless landscape, partaking in both an internal and external journey through God's design.

The warmth of the air completely overtook my focus as the same silent breeze that had first guided me further into the meadow began to blow once more. As the breeze caressed my body a faint spell of exhaustion began to overtake me. With each passing second my strength and energy faded. I was soon brought onto my knees before finally laying down in the bright glow of the sunless sky. My eyes slowly began to shut as I drifted off into a deep slumber.

I opened my eyes only to find myself

alone in my bedroom. I turned my attention to the window. The once bright sunlight of the mid afternoon had been replaced with the deep hue of a twilight sky seeping through my bedroom blinds. I was uncertain of either the time or day during that moment. Standing up from my bed, I walked towards the window and raised the blinds while gazing towards the outside world; a sight that instilled a sense of comfort in my heart that I was home.

As I continued to look upon the world through my bedroom window, the memories of the last conversation I had with The Man rose to the forefront of my mind. I recalled His request to bring forth my revelation to those who were currently experiencing the same depression I had endured. As I meditated on how I could document everything, I instinctively turned my head towards my desk. The papers I had initially planned to use as an artistic channel to escape from the emotional storm within my mind would instead become the vehicle for me to bring my revelation to light.

I understand that my revelation may be divisive as I attempt to navigate areas of theology far beyond my limited knowledge. I know my account may seem illogical and beyond comprehension, but I trust in faith that God will allow it to speak to those who are in

need of answers beyond their own

understanding. For even in these very moments I continue to question the validity of my own account, but nevertheless I'll step out in faith, and trust that God had a purpose and a plan for my life and my revelation.

Even now I'm continuing to seek God's wisdom and knowledge in fulfilling His will for my life. I trust that my revelation will resonate with those who seek His wisdom. The revelation I received by witnessing life, creation, and the world through the eyes of God Himself.

*

18

Pastor William sat in the solitude of his office looking over the rough outline of his intended sermon. His eyes remained locked on a message discussing faith during times of doubt and uncertainty. Though his sermon was intended for his congregation, the true purpose of his message was to reinforce his own trust in God. He remained at his desk proofreading his notes before concluding his day with a quick prayer; one he routinely recited, seeking God's wisdom and a blessing over his sermon and his church.

Before exiting the church, the pastor visited the offices of each of the church's staff members and personally thanked each of them for their patience and efforts during his extended time away. He reflected on his sermon while making his way through the building. Though his conviction in his beliefs was diminishing, his faith remained steadfast. After thanking the fourth and final member of staff, the pastor walked across the foyer, towards the front doors. The light of the setting sun cascaded through the windows, painting the room the same vibrant orange he had seen when he last left the church earlier that week.

    He stepped into his car after leaving his church. He inserted his keys into the ignition and turned on the radio; an effort to drown out the thoughts bombarding his mind. The background noise of the radio hosts discussing the current events of the world accompanied the pastor during his drive home. However, their commentary did little to distract the pastor from his introspection.

    Shortly after pulling into his driveway the pastor shut off the car's engine, allowing the silence to surround him. He opened his door and lifted himself out of the seat before walking across the same dishevelled walkway he often associated with the comfort of his home. Walking passed the kitchen, he could see Grace sitting comfortably on the chesterfield in front of the glow of the television screen. Directly in front of her, situated atop the coffee table was an empty mug and Jacob's papers. Grace's white bookmark sat atop the pages, indicating how she had spent her afternoon.

"Productive day, I take it?" Pastor William greeted his wife.

"You could say that," Grace replied, her eyes still focused on the television screen. "How was your first day back?"

"It was less distracting, if nothing else."

"I'm glad. To be completely honest, you seemed to be getting a little too obsessed over that story." she said, pointing towards the papers resting on the table before her.

"Would I be wrong in assuming you finished it?" he inquired, alluding to the white bookmark atop the pages.

"I knew you were going to be gone all day. I didn't want to get too bored waiting for you to return."

"What did you think of it?"

"I'll let you know when you finish it yourself." Grace replied, "Don't worry, I won't spoil how it ends."

She picked up the remote and pressed the power button, and shut off the light and sound of the television. Rising to her feet, she picked up the papers and her empty mug from the table.

"Dinner will be a little while, why don't you take the opportunity to catch up?" she remarked, handing over Jacob's story to her husband.

"Thank you very much." he said, smiling at his wife's offer.

Grace walked by her husband and kissed his cheek before making her way into their kitchen. He glanced down at the papers in his hand, his black bookmark still protruding from within the pages. He sat down in the same seat of the chesterfield his wife had spent a majority of the day occupying. The warmth of the cushion comforted and relaxed his aged body as he began to flip through the pages before locating his bookmark. Silence soon overtook their home. Both the pastor and his wife were invested in their present activities, with both parties awaiting the other's completion.

The evening passed as Pastor William lost himself in the pages of Jacob's writing. Grace remained in the kitchen occasionally peering into the living room, attempting to gauge her husband's progress through the story. His eyes eventually crossed the final words of Jacob's revelation, reaching the conclusion he had anxiously awaited.

Turning over the final page, he was left with a conclusion he was unable to reject, despite his once steadfast beliefs. Grace peered into the living room once more; her husband sat before her. His head was tilted downward, appearing as though he was in the middle of a prayer. Resting atop Pastor William's lap was Jacob's story; a closed booklet with the two bookmarks set atop of the front page, each one covering half of the title.

Grace continued to look upon her husband, waiting for him to return from his thoughts and prayers. Having read the final chapter herself, Grace was aware of the sort of thoughts potentially stirring around inside her husband's mind. However, unbeknownst to her, the nature of her husband's thoughts were not rooted in defiance or rejection, but of acceptance. Heeding Jacob's advice, Pastor William cast aside himself and his predisposition to accept the divine revelation Jacob had experienced.

He opened his eyes to the booklet resting on his lap. Taking hold of the pages, the pastor removed them from atop his legs and placed them onto the table before him. Rising to his feet, he turned around, only to see his wife peering into the living room, smiling softly. He exchanged a smile of his own before walking towards his wife, eager to share a meal while discussing the revelation he was beginning to accept.

"So you finally made it?" she asked.

"I'm sorry it took so long," he apologized while continuing to smile at his wife.

"I'm just glad you actually managed to get through it all. You were getting antsier as you kept reading."

"I know, and I'm sorry," he apologized, "But I think I'm starting to feel a little better about it now."

"You look a little more chipper than usual."

"I'm glad that you don't see me as some grumpy old man anymore." he said through a smile.

"Oh don't worry, I still do." she teased, "But I'd love to hear all about your thoughts, if you'd be so inclined to discuss it with your old lady."

"I'd like that very much."

"Perfect." Grace smiled as she led her husband into the kitchen.

The aroma of garlic and roasted vegetables filled the air as the couple entered into the kitchen. Two lit candles cast their light onto two plates filled with cooked salmon and roasted vegetables. Grace turned off the lights, allowing the small flames to provide a more romantic atmosphere than the couple would often dine in.

"I thought you would appreciate something a little more special, especially now that you're not trying to wrap your head around that story."

"This is very sweet of you, thank you." The pastor said as he kissed his wife's cheek.

The elderly couple sat down across from each other, basking in the faint light of the candles. Grace prayed a short prayer over their food before indulging in both their dinner and their conversation.

"So what caused your sudden change in attitude?" Grace asked

"I don't necessarily think it was one particular thing, but a culmination of everything I had already read. But I also believe it's more than that."

"What do you mean?"

"I think a lot of it had to do with my willingness to accept something beyond my own understanding. I know you and I have talked about this for a long time, but I believe a lot of it had to do with Jacob admitting his own uncertainty. You and I often discuss things in absolutes, but Jacob's story wasn't like that. He admitted to his own doubts, and God spoke to him regardless. If I want to know God's plans for me when it comes to Jacob's revelation I think I need to shift my focus a little. I had to suspend my own beliefs for the sake of understanding God's role for me in all of this, and I believe that God has revealed to me what that role is."

"And what would that be?" she asked while raising her eyebrows.

"To be Jacob's voice, and to speak to those beyond his reach."

"Do you have any idea as to how you're supposed to do that?"

"No, but I think that if Jacob can have enough faith in God to see the world through His eyes, then I can have enough faith to trust that God will provide me with the means to do what He's asking."

"I have to ask, if you're planning on sharing Jacob's story, do you still believe in God's absolute will? I don't know about you, but I'd find it hard to endorse something I blatantly disagree with."

Pastor William continued to smile at his wife, "Maybe. To be completely honest, after everything that I have read, I'm finding it a little more difficult to continue to hold onto my previous way of thinking. If what Jacob said is true, then perhaps there's more to our lives than I had initially believed."

"Well, I'm glad you're beginning to open your eyes a little. Lord knows I've been trying to do that to you for some time now."

"Oh, I'm well aware of that." Pastor William remarked, "How do you feel about it? You've had a little longer to think it over."

"I think I've started to change my tune as well."

"Why is that?"

"The more I thought about it, the more I agreed with Jacob when he mentioned having a plan within a world of freedom. I used to think that God's intervention was by His choice alone, but if that's the case, then I wouldn't blame someone for thinking that God loves some more than others. If he denied someone a healing for instance, but healed another just because He wanted to, I struggle to see why He'd be seen as a God of endless love. But, on the other hand, if He has a plan with a purpose for us, one we can willingly follow, then it makes sense why He may not always intervene."

"So you now think that there's some truth in what I used to believe?"

Grace raised her hand, squeezing her thumb and index finger together, "Just a little."

"I'll admit that I'm starting to understand what you used to believe a little more as well."

"How so?"

"If God has full control over our lives, then our suffering and condemnation is undeserved. But if God allowed us to have freedom, then I can understand why He would allow pain and sin to exist. If sin is simply a by-product of humanity abandoning God's plan, then we need freedom to abandon His plan in the first place."

"So..." Grace eyed her husband, "What do you think you'll be doing now with your new found freedom?"

"It all depends on where God chooses to lead me. I'll just have to wait for Him I suppose."

"I think that's wise of you."

"If God gave Jacob his revelation for a reason, and I'm to be a part of it, then I'm sure He'll give me some sort of direction." he said, gazing into the flickering light of the candles.

"Speaking of Jacob, do you think you'll be seeing him anytime soon?"

"I honestly don't know." I'd occasionally see his family after the service on Sundays, but their attendance has been rather sporadic lately. But I don't blame them for their absence, given their circumstances."

"I suppose that's natural." Grace lamented.

"Why do you ask?"

"I wouldn't mind having a conversation with him to talk about his story in a little more depth." she replied, looking towards her husband, "But then again, I think you'd have a little more to discuss with him."

"It's possible."

"I think it's more than possible."

Pastor William smiled towards Grace, "I'll be sure to keep an eye out for him and his family on Sunday. If I happen to see them, I'll be sure to let you know."

"It would be appreciated." Grace said.

The light of the flickering candles slowly faded as the couple's dinner reached its conclusion. A comforting silence overtook the once lively conversation shared between husband and wife; one that Pastor William and Grace had found themselves lost within. Though the silence lingered, both the pastor and his wife enjoyed the others' company, absent of the distractions that had occupied their minds. Time seemed to pass slowly in that moment, yet before they even realized it, the evening had arrived. After having returned to his regular routine, exhaustion soon overtook the pastor's body, bringing him to a state of fatigue that quickly spread to Grace, ushering an end to their evening sooner than they would have liked.

Pastor William cleared the table as a thank you for his wife's dinner while she made her way towards the staircase. Having put away the last of the dishes, the pastor followed his wife to the bedroom. As he passed by the living room, in the corner of his eye, he could see the pile of papers resting atop the coffee table. The intrigue and curiosity that initially brought forth his eagerness to read Jacob's revelation had all but settled. A sense of peace finally began to silence the storm that had been dwelling within his mind since he first learned of Jacob's revelation.

    The stillness of the night reflected the calmness in the pastor's mind as he rested his head atop his pillow. The veil of silence continued to cover their home as the night drew on. As he laid down, Pastor William wrapped his arms around his wife in a comforting embrace she then returned. The couple soundly fell asleep, softly cradled within each others' arms. The sun began to rise outside their bedroom window, bathing the world in a warm morning light of the early dawn.

    The days and weeks after Pastor William had concluded Jacob's story fell into a more stable routine. Devoid of distractions, he was once again able to fully commit himself to the needs of his church and the needs of his wife. Every passing Sunday marked another week since Pastor William had first received Jacob's revelation. Yet much to his disappointment, neither Jacob nor his family appeared to be attending the Sunday morning services at their church.

    The initial optimism that Pastor William had in hopes of seeing and conversing with Jacob face-to-face began to wane with each passing Sunday. Unable to contact Jacob's family directly, Pastor William was entirely reliant on their physical appearance in order to converse with them. Although the pastor was unable to speak with Jacob, he continually prayed into God's purpose for his role in Jacob's revelation. While he continued to long for a meaningful conversation with Jacob, he remained focused on what God was asking of him.

Unbeknownst to the pastor, his prayers were soon to be answered. After concluding a Sunday service Pastor William was approached by a young man by the name of David; a member of the pastor's congregation that he saw fairly regularly. However, despite David being a familiar face, the two had yet to formally speak to one another. Following a short greeting, the pastor began to discuss the reason for David's conversation.

"What seems to be on your mind?"

"There was something I was hoping you might be able to help me with, being the pastor and all." his voice shook slightly as he spoke.

"What is it you're seeking?" the pastor inquired.

"I don't really know, I just feel kinda lost. I've been trying to pray about things I'm going through right now, but I just can't seem to find an answer."

"Is there something specific you've been praying into?"

"There's been a lot on my mind," he

stammered while collecting his thoughts, "Mostly I've been praying for God to speak to me, but I can't seem to hear His voice, if He's even speaking at all."

Pastor William raised his eyebrows, "What do you mean?"

"I don't know what to believe at the moment. I've been struggling with my faith for a while now, trying to understand the purpose God has for my life, assuming there even is one to begin with."

"I see."

"I thought that you might be able to help me with all of this. I don't know what I can do, or where else I haven't already looked."

"I think God has been answering your prayers, but maybe not as you would have expected." The pastor alluded through a slight grin, "Unfortunately I don't have very long to talk today. I'm meeting with a couple very shortly to discuss their upcoming wedding, however I'd like to leave you with my home telephone number. Please call me when you have a chance, I believe I have something that you may find rather helpful."

Pastor William grabbed a pen and paper from his shirt pocket and jotted down his phone number.

"Here." The pastor said while offering the paper towards the young man.

David promptly grabbed the paper before reading over the series of numbers written atop the surface.

"Thank you very much." David responded while folding the paper in half and placing it into his pants pocket.

"My pleasure."

David shook the pastor's hand before departing from the building. A faint sense of optimism grew within the young man's heart after his brief meeting with the pastor.

The congregation began to disperse, steadily thinning out following the church's morning service. Pastor William stood quietly in the corner of the room, patiently waiting for Grace to conclude her conversation with one of the church family matriarchs; the last of the church's congregation to remain in the foyer. Grace bid the woman a final goodbye, pleasantly waving to her and her family as they left the building. Pastor William walked across the empty foyer towards his wife, who appeared quite eager to leave the building herself.

"Are you ready to leave?" The pastor asked as he neared Grace.

"Indeed I am." she answered.

Pastor William smiled at his wife before opening the door next to her.

"Please, after you."

"Such a gentleman." Grace responded

as she graciously accepted her husband's gesture.

The couple stepped through the doorway before the pastor turned around and inserted one of the keys into the door's lock, closing the church for another Sunday.

19

"Well Michael, Amy, thank you very much for your time ." Pastor William said, bidding the couple farewell.

"Thank you for meeting with us," Amy replied, "And thank you Grace for your suggestions, though it might be a little late to use them."

"I'm just glad you were willing to listen to me ramble on for a little while."

The car ride home was filled with Grace continuing to discuss her ideas for the upcoming ceremony. The conversation of wedding plans had reignited the passion in her heart for the subject of matrimonies. Though her presence wasn't required, she had gratefully accepted Michael's invitation for her to take part in their meeting.

Upon walking through the door of their home Pastor William made his way towards his study whilst Grace began her weekly routine of cleaning their household. While organizing her bedroom Grace noticed Jacob's story resting atop her husband's nightstand, much to her surprise. The words '*My Story*' written across the center immediately caught her attention. Bending over, Grace picked up the booklet and began to flip through the pages. The emotions she had initially felt when she first read through Jacob's revelation resurfaced as her eyes traversed the hand written paragraphs. Deciding against feeding into her thoughts of God's nature and divinity once more, Grace took hold of the pages and made her way to her husband's study. As she neared the room, she began to overhear the faint sound of a telephone conversation.

"...I'll like to meet with you in my office after the service next Sunday."

Grace was uncertain about the nature of the conversation she was overhearing, but due to her husband's position, scheduled meetings in his office were not a rare occurrence. Grace waited outside the room, slowly flipping through the pages of Jacob's story once more. A brief moment passed before Grace heard her husband bid farewell to his caller and then hang up the phone shortly afterwards. Grace raised her hand towards the door and tapped softly upon the wooden surface.

"Come in, Grace." Pastor William called out.

She opened the door, revealing her husband hunched over his desk.

"I found these on your nightstand." she remarked.

The pastor turned to his wife standing in the doorway, his eyes were immediately drawn to the papers in her hand.

"Do you plan on giving these back to Jacob? she asked.

"When he first gave them to me, it didn't sound like he wanted them to be returned."

"What are you planning on doing with them then?"

"Don't worry, I believe I already know what I'm supposed to do."

"Then I'll leave them in your possession. Just make sure you don't lose your divinely inspired documentation of God's nature and free will among your clutter." she remarked while eyeing the mess slowly building once again in her husband's study.

"It won't happen, trust me."

"Good." Grace said while walking over

and placing the papers atop her husband's desk.

"Now that that's dealt with, I have to ask, are you ready for Saturday?" she inquired.

"Everything has already been taken care of on my part. You don't have to worry about me."

"I know, but I just can't help it."

"I do appreciate your concern, but I'll be fine."

"That's good, I'm just glad that you didn't procrastinate about it. I know how you can be with that sort of thing." she continued to eye the mess on the pastor's desk.

"I know, I know." he responded, "Thank you for your help with everything."

"Well, I'm glad that I was able to be of assistance in your time of need."

The pastor smiled at his wife, before looking down at the papers on his desk.

"Now if you don't mind, I'll return to my cleaning. You're welcome to help me if you'd like." her voice carrying a lilt of wishful optimism that her husband might heed her request.

"We shall see."

"Well, I'll be downstairs if you need me."

Grace took her leave, exiting the room and allowing her husband to return to the solitude of his study. Pastor William turned towards his desk, and gazed over the title of the booklet before turning his attention to the final draft of his officiant speech.

The days of the week seemed to pass by slowly, yet before the pastor realized it, the morning of the wedding had arrived. The loud beeping of an alarm clock broke the silence of dawn, awakening both the pastor and his wife. Pastor William opened his eyes to his bedroom, brightly lit with the warm glow of the early morning sun. After silencing the blaring alarm, the pastor arose from his bed; his body still adjusting to his state of wakefulness. In his absence Grace took full advantage of the additional bed space, a freedom that she always appreciated, even if it meant her husband was no longer lying by her side.

As the morning progressed, Pastor William readied himself for the wedding. Dressed in one of his traditional Sunday morning suits, he made his way into his study, and gathered a few belongings before whispering a farewell to his wife through the cracked open door. He descended the staircase towards the entrance of home. Denying himself breakfast, the pastor opted to dedicate his time towards revising his speech once more before departing his house. Upon exiting his home, he was met with a picturesque summer day; a warm atmosphere befitting of the day a young couple would join hands in the sanctity of marriage. The pastor paused for a brief moment to bask in the light of the sun before entering into his car, placing his belongings onto the passenger seat and driving down the path he had traversed time and time again.

Waiting at the front of the church stood a small group of young men dressed in near identical suits. Among them stood Michael, adorned in a suit fitting a groom, his expression exuded a mix of excitement and nervousness; emotions one would expect of someone soon to be married.

After exiting his car and walking towards the church, the pastor immediately recognized a familiar face in the group of men; Jacob. Upon seeing Jacob's face Pastor William recalled the initial pages of Jacob's revelation, piecing together the relationship Jacob shared with the groom. Deciding against conversing with Jacob before the ceremony, Pastor William briefly introduced himself to the group of groomsmen before unlocking the doors to the church, allowing himself and the men to enter into the building. Jacob was among the last of the men to enter into the foyer. Passing by the pastor, Jacob noticed a familiar looking booklet held within his hand.

Pastor William directed the group of men towards the church's auditorium before briefly returning to his office to unpack his belongings. He quickly prayed in the silence of his office before joining the group of men inside the auditorium. As the minutes passed, a crowd of family and friends slowly began to fill the seats.

      As the wedding music began to play, the guests' conversations faded into silence. What followed was a ceremony filled with the myriad of emotions synonymous with such a joyous and monumental occasion; happiness and elation, optimism and excitement. Laughter was shared and tears were shed throughout the duration of the ceremony. Vows and rings were exchanged as two people started a new journey together. The ceremony reached its conclusion as Pastor William pronounced the union of Michael and Amy Lawson.

      After fulfilling his purpose as the ordained minister, Pastor William lingered in the church's sanctuary as the guests exited into the foyer and then made their way into the room designated for the wedding reception. Standing alone, the pastor attempted to organize his thoughts and questions, hoping for an opportunity to speak with Jacob that he wasn't certain would even occur. As the last of the wedding guests made their way into the reception, the pastor began to walk towards the church's foyer himself.

The celebration commemorating the union of the newlywed couple began soon after the ceremony ended. Emotional speeches were shared as friends and family wished blessings towards Michael and Amy. The music continued to echo throughout the interior of the church as the pastor walked through the church's foyer.

His patience was soon rewarded as he noticed a familiar face standing in the lobby of the church. Jacob, having briefly excused himself from the company and conversation of his fellow groomsmen, decided to take a moment to dwell within the relative silence of the empty entrance hall. The setting sun shone through the windows, casting the last remnants of its light into the church. Pastor William approached Jacob as he remained standing at the window, gazing at the sunset.

"Beautiful, wouldn't you agree?" Pastor William asked, joining Jacob in front of the window.

"It is," he replied.

"I've been wanting to talk to you for some time now."

"I kinda thought so." Jacob said, continuing to look through the church windows, "Once I saw those papers in your hands I knew you'd want to talk sooner or later."

"Would I be wrong in assuming that

Michael and Amy are the childhood friends you wrote about?"

"No, they are."

"I'm surprised you were able to keep in contact for so long."

"It's been difficult, but we've made it work." Jacob reminisced, "Even though they moved away, they both wanted to return here to get married."

"That's very nice."

"It is, and I'm glad that I was able to see them together again."

"It's amazing to think of the ways our paths connect with one another. They separate, diverge and join together again seamlessly. For God to be able to do that is nothing short of incredible"

"It really is."

"I must ask," Pastor William said, turning his head away from the window, towards Jacob, "What was it like?"

"It was eye opening to say the least, seeing everything from God's point of view. I had the power to change the world into whatever I wanted. Even now I still have a hard time believing everything that happened."

"Regardless, I found it to be incredibly insightful."

"I'm glad you appreciated it, although I kinda doubt that everyone will respond the same way."

"Perhaps, but I still believe your story needs to be heard."

"I know God has a purpose for my story," Jacob said, still gazing through the window, "But I also know it won't sit well with everyone. And in all honesty, I'm okay with that. I think He wants to speak to those who struggled like me."

"What about those who find conflict with your revelation, or your interpretation of God's nature? I know that some of the subjects you discussed have the potential to touch a few nerves."

"I'm not too concerned. I'm not claiming to be some prophet. All I know is that God is calling me to simply bring my story to the world. Everyone else will decide whether or not it's for them."

"What would you say to someone who disagrees with your story? I know my wife and I have had our fair share of discussions about these very subjects."

Jacob turned to the pastor, "I'd urge them to read to the very end. Maybe God will speak to them when it's all said and done. I know if I had given up on God, I wouldn't be talking with you about this right now. I know He'll speak to those in need."

"I'm amazed at your faith in all of this."

"I've struggled with my faith for a long time. But after everything that happened, I know God has a purpose for my revelation."

"I agree," the pastor said "I'm a little surprised that this was the first time we've seen each other since you first gave me your story."

"Despite everything I wrote about, I still found it hard to return here. I think a lot of it has to do with the rest of my family and our circumstances. It wouldn't surprise me if they're still struggling with their faith. Though, I think it would be good for them to come back here. Maybe if they come back they'll finally begin to heal."

"Speaking of your family, have they read your story yet?" The pastor inquired.

"Not yet, I think I'd like to give them a little longer before I say anything."

"And why is that?"

"I just don't think they're ready for it just yet. They've been getting better, but I'd like to give them a little bit longer before I bring my story to them.

"How are they doing?"

"As well as you'd expect." he sighed, "Julia has been slowly returning to her old self, and my dad's started reading from his Bible again, but not as often as he used to. Though it's hard to say when he'll return here. And my mom has begun to be a little more expressive since everything happened. I think there's a long journey ahead of us, but I know things will get better."

"That's very encouraging."

"I think so." Jacob smiled

"I just hope when the time comes your story will speak to them as it's spoken to me."

"I hope so as well."

"Jacob! We've been looking for you," A voice called from behind.

Jacob and Pastor William turned around to see Michael urging Jacob to return to the reception.

"Richard wrote a speech and he's excited to start, I don't want you to miss it."

"I'll be right there." Jacob answered "I'm sorry, but I think I'm needed at the moment."

"I understand, thank you for taking the time to talk with me." Pastor William concluded

"You're welcome. I'll see you later." he said as he began to walk towards the reception.

Satisfied with his conversation, Pastor William began to make his way home, having previously entrusted the closing responsibility to a church staff member prior to the wedding. Upon exiting the church, the pastor gazed at the twilight sky before walking across the parking lot towards his car. The last of the sun's light had vanished by the time the pastor returned home.

The pastor's home was quiet and still that evening, an indication that Grace had retired for the night. Following suit, he ascended the staircase towards their bedroom. Eager to rest for the coming Sunday, the pastor removed his suit and readied himself in his night attire. Climbing into his bed, he softly kissed Grace goodnight before returning to the state of sleep he'd been yearning for since the early morning.

Conclusion

Pastor William concluded the morning service with a short prayer, before exiting the sanctuary and making his way through the church corridors towards his office. The sound of the congregation's various conversations filled the air as he neared the door marked *'Pastor William Peterson'*. Opening the door for himself, he made his way towards his desk, pulled out the chair from its place and sat down. Almost immediately, a sudden knock on the door caught his attention.

"Come in." he said, excited to meet with the young man he had spoken to the previous Sunday.

The handle rotated as the door slowly swung open. David stepped into the pastor's office before carefully closing the door behind him, cutting off the growing noise from the church's foyer.

"Please have a seat." Pastor William said, waving his hand towards one of the two chairs situated in front of David.

"Thank you," David responded, while lowering himself into the chair.

"I appreciate you deciding to meet with me today."

"I'm just glad you're willing to listen."

"Is no one else willing to hear you?" The pastor asked.

"It's not that no one else will listen, it's just that no matter how much I pray I can't seem to connect with God. I always feel as though I'm being ignored. I thought that you, being a pastor, might be able to help me with all of this." The emotions in David's voice grew as he spoke, "I just don't understand why nothing is working."

"You're not the first person to speak to me about feeling ignored, and I doubt you'll be the last. I think I have something that may speak to you." Pastor William said as he opened the drawer underneath his desk, pulling out a freshly photocopied booklet of paper.

"What is it?"

"A revelation from someone who has faced the same struggles you're enduring, who was given an answer that may resonate with you. Please take it." Pastor William said as he handed David the papers in his hand. David looked at them, uncertain as to what exactly he was holding. Within his hands he held a booklet with two words written across the center of the first page; *'My Story'*.

Made in the USA
Monee, IL
15 December 2020